A Small Dog Story

GW01048770

Based on true events   a

little terrier, big in pe   a

puppy, find out how she survives as a stray with the

help from the new friends she meets along the way, and

from Benni the streetwise dog. Her adventures include

life in Dublin, how she comes to be chosen as a

Hearing Dog and her travels to England for training.

Humorous, hopeful and happy, royalties will be

donated to Hearing Dogs for Deaf People. Woof!

A Small Dog Story

Dedicated to all Hearing Dogs
and those who love them

Published by Mike Moss 2019

Second Edition 2019

Text and Cover Graphics © Mike Moss 2019

Illustrations © Shirley Pickin 2019

All rights reserved. No part of this publication may be reproduced, stored in or introduced into a retrieval system, or transmitted in any form, or by any means, (electronic, mechanical, photocopying, recording or otherwise) without the prior written permission of the publisher.

MY STORY

Chapter 1 – A Bad Start

Lost! It's so, *so* scary being lost and a stray.

Imagine! You have no home, you don't know where your mum is, nor your sisters and brothers. You're soaking wet, cold and hungry, with no idea where your next meal is coming from, and completely lost. As lost as a black canary down a coal mine at midnight. As if that wasn't bad enough, you are only six months old and being chased by two angry dogs. That's where my story starts – as a stray dog in Dublin, running like there's no tomorrow. There are sad bits (these happen without warning, so if you don't like sad bits then stop reading now!), some nail-biting bits and some jolly bits, in fact quite a few jolly bits so it probably is worth carrying on reading, and the ending is...well, you decide when you reach it.

When I say sad bits, I mean like the time I was trotting sadly down the alley after running away from

Sinéad's house, lost again and trying to find my way back, when I saw an open gate. I poked my head through the gap and saw two bowls of scrumptious looking dog food, lying by the door of a large blue house. Well, I was hungry, dogs never refuse food and I like to eat, so that's what I did. Halfway through the first bowl, licking my lips, I heard a deep growl behind me. Still chewing, I turned my head to see a bull terrier lumbering around the corner of the house.

It stopped and glared at me in a way only bull terriers can. Then it looked at the bowl. Slowly, I turned to face it, still licking my lips. Oops. Tasty but trouble, I thought.

'Wadya doin', kid? That's Cumberland's dinner,' he growled, 'Cumberland, come 'ere!'

Immediately, from behind him, trotted a really chunky, round, brown sausage dog. His charcoal coloured ears almost scraped along the ground and he was so fat he looked like a huge salami on little legs.

''E's eating your dinner, Cumberland, 'e is.'

Cumberland narrowed his eyes and gave me a snarlie from the corner of his mouth. Sausage dogs are wimps except when they are with other dogs, especially big or strong dogs. Then they can be fierce.

Cumberland growled and moved to my left, while the bull terrier started to edge around to my right.

'Sorry,' I apologised, holding my ground to face them off, because I am a plucky, brave sort of dog. 'Look, I'm lost and I was really famished,' I continued, hoping they would understand.

They didn't. They kept moving slowly, growling, eyes fixed firmly on me, edging either side of me.

Time to go I thought, so I did. I turned and ran back into the alley. Phew, that was close I said to myself as I trotted away. I turned to look behind me.

Suddenly Cumberland darted through the gate, followed closely by the bull terrier.

'There she is, Bull, let's get her!'

I took off like a streak of lightning, running down the alley.

I'm a fast runner and Cumberland was cumbersome and slow, his tummy almost bouncing along the ground as he waddled and ran. Bull, on the other hand, was quick. I could hear his paws pounding the pebbles and his snorts and breathing close behind me. I didn't look back, but I knew he wasn't far behind. I expected him to bite my tail any minute.

'I'll teach you to eat our food,' he grimaced in his gravelly, growly voice.

I ran faster, panting now. Down the street, along the pavement, dodging and zigging and zagging between people's legs, around lamp posts and under shopping bags to cries of 'oi' and 'watch out!' following me. I ran across the entrances to alley ways, picking up the different smells as I passed a row of shops – a baker, a chemist, a book shop, a drain, a strong perfume - always with Bull's heavy panting not far behind.

I turned a corner, but the street was very busy, slowing me down so I darted right, into an alley. Bull couldn't turn in time and skidded on beyond the alley. I knew it was only a matter of time before he turned and continued the chase. I ran down the side of the alley until, uh oh! The way was barred, literally, by two big wrought iron barred gates. It was an entrance into the park, but the gates were shut.

I was cornered.

I turned to find Bull trotting triumphantly down the alley, snarling, slowing, his black beady eyes fixed on mine. He knew I was trapped. Cumberland was nowhere in sight.

'Hey, I'm sorry, let's talk about this,' I suggested, in a 'let's be friends' sort of way, not a wimpy way of course.

'When I've bitten you to bits, you pompous, food pinching pooch' snarled Bull.

Just then Cumberland came running around the corner, panting like a wheezy organ. He slowed, stopped to catch his breath then waddled up beside Bull. They looked at each other and started to advance together.

I was doubly trapped.

I backed away until I could feel the cold iron bars against my back.

'How was I going to escape from this?', I thought.

But, dear reader, if I carry on from here, I will reach the end of my story before I've told you the beginning or the middle. So, let me start at the beginning and introduce myself.

Aoo-oo-ohh-f! which means 'hi, nice to meet you.' My name is Izzie. I'm a little dog, five years old as I write this, a girl, grey and furry, with a little white patch on my chest and I'm a little terrier. I have black pointy ears and a moist, button nose and, like most terriers, I'm courageous, adventurous and like chasing little animals, especially furry ones. By the time I was one and a half years old I had had enough adventures to fill a book! This book, in fact. But let me start at the beginning of my story, a few years ago in Dublin.

Chapter 2 – My Early Life

I was born one February in Dublin, the capital city of the Republic of Ireland. My mum was a Kerry Blue terrier called Delilah and I had two sisters, called Lizzie and Dizzie, and two brothers, called Whizzie and Bizzie. I never knew my dad, he was some sort of terrier too, so we were, as they say at the dog shows, mixed breed and looked a bit different from our mum. The big, terraced house we lived in was near the centre of the city, but we were only allowed in the kitchen or the back yard and garden, which were surrounded by high walls and a big, black metal gate with bars. On most days we would run around the yard and stick our noses out of the bars, sniff the air and play games like Jump the Dog.

'Quick,' whispered Whizzie, 'I can smell that young collie coming.'

'Hide behind the wall, 'Bizzie whispered.

Then, when the collie and its owner came past, we would jump out and bark. The owner always gave a jump which made us laugh, as he had a big tummy and it wobbled up and down.

'Daft dogs,' grunted the collie's owner, rattling his walking stick in the bars of the gate to scare us away.

'Good one,' beamed the collie, 'but smelt you a mile off.'

Across the street was The Park. It was huge. It stretched as far as the eye could see, although being quite small and low down we couldn't actually see very far. We longed to be able to go and run around the trees and through the bushes.

'You're not allowed,' explained mum gently. 'You're too little and will get lost, or you might fall in the Grand Canal or the River Liffey.'

Sometimes mums are no fun!

We were part of a pack that included what my mum called 'people' and my first few months were spent in the Keane pack. There was Ma Keane, Pa Keane and the two little Keanes, Josie and Joe. I was a little bit scared of Pa Keane, who was a big man with lots of hair on his face. He shouted a lot and his favourite meal was Keanes on toast – how scary is that![1]

Joe Keane, the boy, used to tease us and try to frighten us. He liked to make us jump in fright by making loud noises and bangs, or chasing us with the hoover. Joe decided my reaction to the hoover was hilarious so, when the adults weren't about and his friends were there, he would start the hoover and chase me with it. It made them laugh. I didn't like Joe as much as Josie, but he wasn't all bad and he was one of the pack after all.

I think most people know dogs don't like loud noises and bangs, well I certainly don't! And now you know I hate hoovers and, by the way, whirry things like lawn mowers and hair dryers too. This all started when I was little. Ma Keane was doing the housework (something we dogs don't bother to do, we let the humans do it for us) and she started the hoover right next to me. Well, I was dozing and jumped in fright, took one look at the noisy thing heading in my direction, ran across the kitchen and jumped through the doggy flap in the back door into the yard. Luckily it didn't follow me.

---

[1] I think Izzie means beans on toast – I expect she misheard

I heard Joe laughing his head off and Ma Keane call out 'Sorry, Izzie, I didn't mean to scare you, it's only a hoover!'

Mum jumped through the flap, came up to me and put her paw on my back. 'My, you're trembling all over.'

I whined back.

Gently, she licked my nose and sat down beside me until I had stopped trembling.

'Come on,' she suggested kindly, 'let's go and sniff the garden.'

'Good idea,' I replied. I love sniffing, maybe I could pick up a new scent, I thought.

I learnt at an early age that sniffing is what dogs do best. Dogs like me smell a lot. I don't mean we are smelly or pongy, just that we are really good at using our noses. We can smell the faintest of scents, whiffs or pongs and we rely on our sense of smell more than our eyes to find food. Sniffing is important to dogs for a number of reasons:

1. To find things to eat, like chips and chocolate dropped on the pavement.

2. To check out another dog, to see if we should be friends.

3. To see if other dogs have marked my territory, so I can mark it again with my scent.

4. To sniff my pack when they return home, to see where they have been.

5. To find small furry things to chase, like cats and squirrels.

The first smell I can remember was my doggy family. I was curled up in the den with my brothers and sisters and mum and became aware of my nose wrinkling up and taking in that smell. It's a homely, earthy, doggy smell that all little dogs like. The importance of sniffing is summed up in one of my favourite poems which goes like this:

> What is this life if, full of care
>
> We have no time to sniff and stare?
>
> No time to sniff beneath the boughs
>
> And stare as long as sheep or cows.[2]

When I'm out for a 'walk', as my pack call it, or a 'good hunt, scavenge and chase' as I call it, my nose is usually a few millimetres off the ground checking for faint scents. When I find one, I like to follow it until I

---

[2] Izzie has slightly misquoted the well known poem 'Leisure' by W.H. Davies, but then she is a little dog without much education so we need to make allowances.

find the source (like a cat or some dropped food) or until it fades away. Following scents is like learning with your nose. I learn lots of new things this way and I'm proud to say that I can distinguish each dog and cat in the neighbourhood by its scent. I will sniff around to find a good place to poop or check where other dogs have been so I can lay my own scent at the same place, just to show them whose territory it really is. I will do this a few times on each hunt and do it at the same place each day.

Anyway, living with the pack in Dublin was fun. Mum, Ma Keane and Josie made sure we were fed and groomed. We spent the time playing, running, rushing and rolling around the kitchen, yard and garden. Often Pa Keane was annoyed that there were five of us pups, especially when we were being too noisy or, as he often did, almost tripping up over us, spilling his beer.

One day, a few weeks after we were born, we heard a big argument in the hall. I crept up to the kitchen door and poked my head around the corner. All four Keanes were in the hall. The little Keanes, Josie and Joe, were sitting on the stairs, head in hands.

'What,' demanded Pa Keane crossly, pointing at the kitchen door 'are we going to do with all these pups?'. I ducked back inside in case he saw me.

'Can't we keep them all?' I heard one of the little Keanes cry.

Pa Keane snorted, 'you have got to be joking. It's the canal for them, more like.' Josie gasped.

'Don't worry, dears, I think your father is joking. We can sell them or give them away,' explained Ma Keane. I poked my head around the door again, no-one was looking in my direction.

'Well, they won't be worth much as they're mongrels, but it's worth a try. The children can sort it out,' decided Pa Keane in his 'and that's the end of it' tone of voice.

'I don't think the children are old enough to be responsible for selling the pups, 'replied Ma Keane, keeping the debate open.

The discussion continued and it developed into another argument. Mum, standing just behind me, was looking worried. When the Keanes argued, which they often did, things started to fly. When she was little, she had been thrown out of the kitchen window during such an argument. Luckily it was open at the time.

She had told all of us to hide when these arguments flared up, so we did. I hid under the pile of washing. It was a pretty safe place as, more often than not, the washing lay in piles for days on end before being put into the washing machine. It was a bit whiffy, but dogs don't mind that sort of thing.

The argument continued until it was decided we would be sold, if possible, when we were eight or nine weeks old, which we almost were, and that Ma Keane would sort it out. Josie and Joe would help. Apparently, we had to be weaned and wormed before we were sold.

'Weaned and wormed?' squeaked Bizzie, puzzled.

'Weaning means when you start eating food out of a bowl and worming is just a pill,' explained mum.

'I don't want to be sold,' whined Lizzie sadly, hanging her head, 'I want to stay here with mum and the rest of you.'

Mum licked her nose and said she was sad to hear we would be sold. She gently explained it was very common for puppies to be given to other people and that nearly always they would be looked after nicely, given lots of chewy treats, cuddles and more.

'Wow!' beamed Whizzie, pricking up his ears and bouncing up and down, 'lots of treats? Chewy ones?'

'Lots, and very chewy, I expect,' replied mum perking up.

'And will our coats be groomed nicely?' asked Lizzie, 'I love it when my coat is groomed!'

'Oh, yes, I'm sure you will be groomed regularly, dear.'

I was alarmed at the idea of my family being broken up, but it felt like we had no choice.   Where would I end up? It was a worry.

Chapter 3 - My Family Move on

Over the next few days some of the Keane's friends came by to look at us. Henry came first. He was a plump boy, about eight, who always had a lollipop in his mouth. When he finished one, he took another from his pocket. He seemed to have a pocketful of purple lollies.

Henry's mum was a small, petite lady with brown hair and kind brown eyes. She wore a flowery blouse, jeans and pink trainers with clean white laces. She smelt of lavender. She was all smiles and looked very friendly.

'Well,' she exclaimed, looking at us little dogs lined up, sitting in a neat row on the kitchen floor, 'aren't they sweet and well behaved.'

'Look, mum,' mumbled Henry through his lollipop and pointing at Whizzie, 'that one looks like an Ewok! Can I have him?'

I didn't know what an Ewok was (and I still don't[3]) but I'm sure Whizzie looked just like a puppy, not an Ewok. If he was an Ewok he wouldn't be a dog, would he?

'All right,' replied Henry's mum, patting Whizzie on the head and tickling his chin, 'we'll have Whizzie please, Mrs Keane.'

Whizzie was pleased to be chosen but was sad to be going.

'See you in the park when we're older,' Whizzie called, as he was picked up by Henry. Henry put Whizzie in his satchel so just his head was poking out.

'Enjoy the treats,' I called after him.

'Let's hope they're really chewy,' came the muffled reply from the satchel as the front door was closing.

Our next visitor was Amelia, a goofy girl with ginger hair, bunches and freckles. Her father was small and smelt of stale cigarettes and beer, just like Pa Keane. He was bald, wore tatty shoes and had a chesty

---

[3] Of course fans of Star Wars will know that Ewoks are a species of furry, teddy-bear-like hunter-gatherers that inhabit the forest moon of Endor, somewhere in another galaxy far, far away.

cough. Amelia filled the kitchen as soon as she entered.

'I want a girl dog!' stomped Amelia.

'Of course you do, poppet,' replied Amelia's dad, scratching his brown beard.

I took an instant dislike to Amelia and her Dad. I hoped they wouldn't buy one of us. Life with them wouldn't be fun, but what could I do? I thought hard while Amelia looked at us, her hand on her chin.

'Lizzie, Dizzie, growl if she goes near you,' I whispered urgently.

'What? Why...?' came the surprised response.

'They're not nice people,' I murmured insistently, pretending to lick my paw.

Amelia asked bossily, 'Which one's a girl? I want a girl dog!'

'These three here are the girls, dear,' replied Ma Keane.

'Oh, I like that one,' she chirped, moving towards Lizzie. Lizzie gave a low growl and bared her teeth. Amelia stopped dead in her tracks and turned to look at her dad.

'Is she fierce?' asked Amelia's dad. He coughed.

'Oh dear,' replied Ma Keane, 'I don't know why she's growling. Lizzie, stop that at once!'

'It's all right,' announced Amelia, 'I wanted this one anyway,' she pouted, turning towards Dizzie.

Ma Keane smiled, 'A good choice. She's very sweet natured, in fact....'

Ma Keane stopped as Dizzie started to growl too. Amelia looked at her dad. Her dad looked at Amelia, then Dizzie, then Ma Keane.

'I don't know what you are up to, missus,' he fumed, 'but these dogs aren't fit for small children. I've a good mind to report you. Com' on, Amelia, we'll look elsewhere.' They turned to go and left, slamming the front door as they went.

'Oh dear,' said Ma Keane, frowning at Lizzie and Dizzie, 'I don't know what that was all about. What's got into you two, then?'

Lizzie and Dizzie looked at me. I just cocked my head to one side, looked at the ceiling and wagged my tail. Mum winked at me from her basket.

A few days passed and no-one else came to view me or the others. Maybe Amelia and her dad had spread the word about the fierce pack of dogs up for sale. Mum thought it was because it was raining 'cats and dogs' all weekend and who would want to buy a dog when it's raining cats and dogs anyway. I think she was making a joke.

The next day the sun came out and, sure enough, the doorbell rang in the late afternoon. Ma Keane answered it as I poked my head around the kitchen door to see who it was. There on the doorstep was a blond, angelic looking girl and a cheerful man in a smart, stripy suit, smiling broadly.

'We've come about the dogs,' they spoke almost in unison, 'have you any left?' added the little girl, fidgeting with her hands as she stood on the doorstep and adding, 'please'.

'Oh, yes, dear, we have four left, come in and have a look,' replied Ma Keane.

The little girl came in first, almost skipping down the hall, followed by her dad.

'I have a list of things to look for in puppies,' announced the little girl, waving a piece of paper with a neatly handwritten list on it.

Izzy the Girl's list for buying puppies

1. Watch the litter and how the pups interact with each other. An active, playful pup is good, but not one that is too dominant or overbearing with its litter-mates.

2. Do a general visual health check. They should be nice and round - not fat, and certainly not skinny.

3. Look for a confident pup that struts up to you with head held high and tail wagging with excitement. A bit of a cheeky lick on the hand is ok.

4. Check that the pup's ears, gums, teeth and rear end look OK.

5. Check for bright eyes and a shiny and clean coat.

6. Pick the puppy up, hug it and cradle it. It is not a good sign if it squeals and wriggles and doesn't settle down.

7. Touch the puppy all over its body, including paws, mouth and ears to monitor the reaction. A puppy which has been handled from an early age won't have any problem with you doing this.

'Well, you are organised,' replied Ma Keane approvingly, 'I hope ours pass the test! Izzie, Dizzie, Lizzie, Bizzie, come here. Oh, there you are, Lizzie.'

Lizzie was the first to appear, wagging her tail. She had heard the little girl skipping down the hall and thought she sounded fun. Lizzie went up to her and sat down, her tail swishing left to right over the hall tiles, helping to clean the hall by moving little bits of fluff to the side.

'This one looks a nice dog, doesn't she, Izzy?' asked the cheery man cheerfully. I pricked up my ears, was he talking to me? He wasn't looking at me.

'Oh, is your name Izzy?' asked Ma Keane, 'this little grey puppy is called Izzie too!'

'Well, well,' chuckled the cheery man, 'We can't have two Izzies in the house, that would be very confusing, we might mix up their dinners - or worse!' he chuckled again.

'My dad's so funny,' giggled Izzy, as she knelt on the floor, Lizzie licking her hand. Izzy looked Lizzie all over and picked her up. Lizzie licked her cheek.

'Can we have this one, Dad, Lizzie? She's nice.' Lizzie was now sniffing Izzy's ear. 'Have you been through your list, Izzy?' replied Izzy's dad, adding to

Ma Keane, 'she's a good one for doing her research carefully. It helps her learn and stand on her own two feet.'

'Very commendable, I'm sure,' replied Ma Keane turning to look sideways into the sitting room, 'I wish my two could do the same.'

Joe, lying on the sitting room sofa playing a game on his X-box, looked up briefly at the three of them before going back to his game.

Izzy sat down with Lizzie and went through her list, ticking off each item as she completed it.

'She passes everything on the list, Dad. Can we have Lizzie?'

'OK, Izzy, Lizzie it is,' he beamed.

Izzy brought out a bag of cheesy treats and gave one to Lizzie.

Cheesy treats! We all crowded around Izzy, looking at her expectantly.

'Can the others have one?' she asked Ma Keane, holding up her bag.

'Of course, dear, that's very kind of you,' responded Ma Keane as Izzy gave us all a treat.

'You'll be well looked after with Izzy,' I whispered to Lizzie.

'I've brought a lead,' explained Izzy, clipping it onto Lizzie's collar. 'Come on then Lizzie, let's go home.'

Izzy's dad gave Ma Keane some money as the three of them went down the hall and out into the street. As the front door opened, the sunshine streamed in, outlining everyone in gold. Lizzie, her face alight, turned and gave a final wooo-af goodbye before disappearing down the street. Ma Keane shut the door. We were all very quiet. Who's next, we wondered.

Later that day Dizzie was sold to a grumpy old man in suede shoes and bright yellow socks (dogs notice this sort of thing, being a lot closer to the ground). He argued and argued about the price with Ma Keane.

'It's for the missus,' he told Ma Keane, 'to keep her company, like, now she's housebound.'

'Fair enough,' she replied, 'hope she enjoys him. Don't forget she'll need two walks a day,' finally taking a handful of crumpled ten Euro notes from the man.

Then there was only Bizzie and me left. Our last visitor was a little boy, Jimmy, with her mother.

Jimmy looked at me, then Bizzie.

'Is that one very old?' he asked, pointing at me.

'No, they're the same age,' replied Ma Keane in a puzzled tone.

'Then why is it grey and this one black?'

'That's just the colour they are, dear,' explained Ma Keane.

'Well, I don't want one that looks old. I want the black one!'

'Sure you do,' replied Jimmy's mum in a snooty accent, 'is it toilet trained yet? I don't want one that isn't! It is? Oh good. We'll take the black one then.'

So then there was one, me.

When I snuggled up that night it was different now there was only me and mum left. The den smelt different too. My mind was racing, and I couldn't stop thinking about my brothers and sisters and whether I would ever see then again. Eventually I fell into a fitful sleep and dreamed that the whole pack was reunited in a huge house and we had good fun playing games like nip, tag and rough and tumble like we always used to. At food time we were given huge piles of treats but every time we tried to eat them they disappeared. I woke up the next morning ready to play but, when I saw only two food bowls, I remembered there was no one left to play with. I ate my breakfast on my own and wondered what the future had in store for me. I was soon to find out.

Chapter 4 - New tricks

The Keanes decided not to sell me but to keep me as a pet. Mum was pleased. So was I. Josie and Joe thought I should be trained. Training is an important part of a dog's life. After all, without proper training how would my people know when to feed me or take me out for a walk? This is why it is so important that dogs train their people properly. Of course, people like to think they are training dogs and it works better if one plays along with this idea.

The key thing to remember about training is to win as many treats as possible. There is an art in doing this.

'Mum,' called Josie, 'can we train Izzie?'

'Of course you can,' came the reply from the kitchen, 'what are you going to train her to do?'

Chase squirrels, I thought hopefully, or birds maybe, although I didn't think I needed much training in this field, though I'm sure it all helps.

'Erm, we could train her to fetch maybe.'

'Good idea, do that then.'

'Yeah, and train her to fetch my slippers and paper while you're at it,' came Pa Keane's sarcastic voice from the sitting room, where he was sitting reading the adverts in the Dublin News.

'I think we'll start with a ball,' Joe called out.

So Josie and Joe started throwing a tennis ball and shouting 'fetch'. I was puzzled at first. I ran over to where the ball had landed and sat down next to it, waiting for a treat.

'No, no, stupid dog, bring the ball here,' shouted Joe.

Leaving the ball where it landed, I ran up to Joe and sat down in front of him, wagging my tail as fast as a helicopter about to take off.

'Here. Treat?' I woofed expectantly.

'Stupid dog!' snapped Joe, walking off, 'we're never going to train it.'

'It's OK, Izzie,' murmured Josie, tickling me behind my ears, 'Joe has the attention span of a gnat. It's just you and me! Let's try something else. Every time you sit when I say 'sit!' I give you a treat,' she said holding up the treat bag. I wagged my tail.

'Treat?' I woofed.

'Here goes then!'

Fourteen treats later, Josie reckoned I had been trained to sit. I found it was best to play stupid sometimes, so she was more likely to give me treats when I did what I was meant to do.

'Josie, lunch is ready,' called Josie's mum from the back door.

Josie ran in, leaving me in the yard.

I trotted back to my den for a rest – it can be tiring work winning treats. Mum was lying there, dozing.

'What did you learn today then, Izzie?' asked my mum, opening one eye.

'How to sit.'

'Oh,' mum paused thoughtfully, 'useful. I hope you managed to earn lots of treats.'

'I did and I saved one for you,' dropping the treat from my mouth in front of her.

'Thanks, Izzie, you are a kind dog,' she murmured, as she ate the treat and went back to dozing.

I curled up beside her; she was so soft and cosy, and listened as Josie explained to anyone who would pay attention how she had trained me to sit.

Chapter 5 – Lost!

With my brothers and sisters gone, we settled into a new routine. Josie and Joe would stroke my tummy, groom and train me and take me for walks with my mum in the park, by the River Liffey or to the Grand Canal. They liked to go up to the edge of the canal and peer down into the water and at all the colourful boats coming through the locks. We were always amazed at what people kept on top of their boats; bicycles, chairs, TV aerials, solar panels, plants, bags of coal and wood for the stove, boathooks, dog kennels and all sorts of things. Mum told me to keep away from the edge because, if I fell in, I wouldn't be able to climb out and would drown.

The days were becoming warmer and I enjoyed the park. There were other dogs, lots of good scents to follow and, sometimes, a discarded burger, piece of pizza or the odd chip to wolf down. I was always on a lead but I didn't mind too much because I knew I had a lot to learn.

Then, one day, Josie Keane called me over, 'Come on, Izzie, I'll take you off your lead and you can have a little run about. Remember, when I say 'Come!' you must come straight back, just like you've been trained to do.'

Mum warned me, 'Don't go too far, keep us in sight.'

I mooched off a bit but kept the Keanes and mum in sight for a while. It was exciting being off the lead. I could wander and pick up scents then follow them. I looked up to see the Keanes playing with their yellow Frisbee, watched by mum. Then, just as I was about to go back, a movement at the bottom of a nearby tree caught my eye. A small furry thing with a big bushy tail. Squirrel!

In the blink of an eye, I was chasing it.

It ran underneath a bush and out of the other side, jumped up a tree and started climbing. I arrived at the base of the tree just behind it. I jumped up but it was too quick for me, so I stood there, front paws on the trunk, and barked and barked.

'Come on,' I barked, 'let's play chase down here. Dogs can't climb trees!'

I waited but the squirrel didn't reply and had disappeared.

I looked around for another, but they must have all been hiding so I decided to go back to mum. But which way was it? My pack had disappeared when I rushed into the undergrowth. For a moment I thought I might be lost but then I realised I could follow my own scent back, so that's what I did.

As I approached mum and the Keanes I could see they were talking to someone. It was Whizzie and his new owner, Henry. Henry had a purple lollipop in his mouth.

Mum was cross. 'I told you to stay close, not go running off. What were you chasing anyway?'

'A squirrel. It ran up a tree.'

'Of course it did. They live up trees. You'll never catch a squirrel up a tree.'

'I know, mum, but it's fun trying, isn't it?'

'I suppose so,' she conceded, smiling at me and patting me on the paw.

Just then Whizzie jumped on me and pushed me over.

'Hiya, Izzie, how are you doing?' he asked, as we went rolling over, picking up bits of newly mown lawn in our fur.

'Good to see you Whizzie, let's play tag, you run first.'

Whizzie ran off with me in pursuit. He feinted left and went right then came up behind me as I skidded round.

'You're on!' he shouted, running off.

We played in the park a while longer, barked 'hi' to a few passing dogs, tried to play catch the Frisbee and watched the world go by. Eventually Josie told us it was time to go back for lunch, so we said goodbye to Whizzie and Henry and we all trotted happily back home.

It was the school holidays so the children would often go to play in the park and take us with them. It was usually sunny (after all we dogs don't like going out in the rain). I was allowed to roam freely provided I didn't go too far and I came back when called. I would smell the flowers and the bushes, which were starting to come to life in the new warmth of spring and the longer, sunny days. My favourite flowers were the daffodils. I would chase the squirrels up the trees, look for scraps of food to eat and play tag with some of the other dogs. It was great fun, but it wasn't to last.

The day it happened was the last day of the school holidays. I know this because Joe was complaining all the way to the park about going back to school the next day.

'I think I'll come down with an illness tomorrow' he was saying, 'something nasty like start-of-term-itis.'

'I think Ma will spot that one a mile off,' laughed Josie.

When we arrived, the children started playing with some friends. Henry was there, with lollipop, but Whizzie wasn't well so he had had to stay at home. I wrinkled my nose and started sniffing. It wasn't long before I found a squirrel under a bush and the chase was on! It was quite a way to the nearest tree, so I had a good run before it shinnied up the tree. Then I saw another a little way off so off I dashed towards it. Quickly, it dived behind a huge tree. I went tearing round after it when CRASH! I had run into something big, long, soft and furry and we went rolling over and over. We both recovered our feet about the same time.

I had crashed into a big greyhound and it was angry, maybe it was chasing the squirrel too.

'What the.....,' it growled as it stood up, 'I'll teach you to knock me over.'

I was a bit confused about why he wanted to teach me to knock him over as I had already done so, but as he was angry, I thought it best to scarper, even though I am a plucky, brave little dog.

'Sorry,' I called, running off. The greyhound took off after me.

Now everyone knows greyhounds are fast but, I can tell you from experience, Izzies are indomitable individuals and can run very fast when chased by greyhounds, even though I admit the one chasing me was quite old. I ran through the trees and dodged past the pond, sending the ducks quacking and flying off in alarm in all directions as I went. I charged towards the bushes on the other side, past a large monument, around it then up the steps of the monument, down the other side and back towards the bushes. My youth, energy and fleetness of foot were telling and I could hear the elderly greyhound struggling for breath. I ran into a rhododendron bush, just starting to blossom and flower pink and orange. The branches became thicker, slowing me down. Then I came to a tangled mass and squeezed through, doubting the greyhound would or could follow. It couldn't.

It stopped and growled, out of sight, hidden by the leaves, 'I'll get you next time, kid.'

'I didn't mean to knock you over,' I replied.

'Sprinter! SPRINter!' came a muffled, out of breath voice. 'Sprinter, come HERE. Where is that stupid dog? SPRINTER!'

I heard Sprinter turn and walk back to his master.

'There you are! Bad dog for running off,' berated Sprinter's owner. He was cross and I could hear him chastising Sprinter as they disappeared into the distance.

I thought I ought to go back to mum and the Keanes, so I waited two or three minutes to make sure the coast was clear. I started to move away when suddenly I couldn't move. I pushed and pulled and heaved and twisted but I was stuck. My collar was caught on something. Concerned, I started to whine then bark for help. That's when it started to rain. It started as a pitter patter on the leaves, then it became an incessant drumming that drowned out all other noises. It was, as the Keanes liked to say, raining cats and dogs. I struggled to free myself, but it was no good. I was stuck.

I barked, 'mum, help, mum, I'm here.' I barked and barked but the rain was so noisy I don't think anyone heard. Soon it turned into hail stones and I could hear the hail hissing among the heather and bushes. Luckily, I was quite sheltered under the thick branches and leaves; even so I started to feel damp, then wet and wetter still.

I suppose Joe and Josie and mum looked for me, but I spent the rest of the day stuck in the bushes, becoming wetter and wetter and colder and colder and hungrier and hungrier. Scared now, I started to whine.

When it started to go dark, I decided I must try to free myself, so I wriggled, jiggled, pushed, pulled and twisted. It was tiring and it made my neck hurt. I was about to give up when suddenly I was free. My collar had snapped and I was free! I found my way out of the bush and circled around so I could pick up my scent and find my way back home. But disaster! I soon realised that the heavy rain had washed all traces of it away. There was no scent! I looked around. It was dark. I had never felt so lonely and disorientated. I had never been out in the dark. I was wet, cold, hungry and LOST!

Chapter 6 - New Friends

I sat for a while trying to work out what to do. Maybe Josie and Joe were looking for me. I couldn't see anyone about. In the distance I heard ducks quacking and the whoosh and rumble of distant traffic, but I couldn't hear anyone calling my name.

I wasn't sure which direction to take. I could turn left or right or go straight ahead. There is probably one right way and two wrong ways, I thought. Then I heard a voice, my ears pricked up, maybe it was Josie or Joe. No, it was a deeper voice, which became voices, maybe two or three. They sounded cheerful. I turned left in their direction towards an underpass, turning a corner. Suddenly I saw two huge shadows, flickering on the wall. I froze. Giants! I slunk back behind a large bush, ready to run. Just then I caught the aroma of sausages cooking. I edged closer, keeping behind the bush. I peered around it and saw three tramps sitting around a small fire, cooking sausages.

They weren't giants after all, despite their huge shadows on the wall. A spurt of fat shot out of a sausage onto the fire, causing it to flare and light up the faces of the tramps, who were laughing.

'They smell good, P-p-pat.'

'Spar's best! Fell into my pocket, they did, so. Forgot to pay, I did,' chuckled Pat, turning a row of sausages on a stick over a fire. 'Three for you and Michael and four for me.'

'Fair enough,' laughed Michael, 'but here is the best bit,' and from under his long, shabby, grey overcoat he bought out a French loaf. 'Fell off the baker's cart, it did. Rescued it, I did!'

They all laughed.

'P-P-Pat, Michael, 'whispered the third man, 'we got company.'

'Where?' asked Pat, lifting his head.

'The Gardai[4]!' exclaimed Michael, looking round as he started to stand up.

'No-oo, look,' replied the third man, turning to point at me.

---

[4] The Gardai (pronounced Gar-dee) are the Irish Police. A policeman is a Garda. You probably knew that anyway.

'Bejesus, Murphy, you had me going! It's only a small dog! And the little blighter's shivering, so.'

It's true. I was shivering from cold and fear. By instinct I lifted my right front leg, ready to run.

'Give him a sausage, Pat, you've got a spare one,' suggested Michael.

'Spare indeed, you can give him a share of your bread then, Michael.'

'Alright, then,' replied Michael, breaking off a piece of bread and holding it out to me, 'Com'on, little 'un,' he smiled, waving a chunk of bread at me.

I slowly, cautiously, edged forward, keeping one eye on the bread and the other on Michael and the others. My hunger, and the hope that they might know that the Keanes were looking for me, spurred me forward.

I took the bread gently from his fingers, took it back to the bush and chewed it quickly, all the time keeping a close eye on the three of them.

'He's hungry,' chuckled Michael.

'Dogs are always hungry[5],' replied Murphy.

---

[5] This is true.

Pat threw me a sausage. I LOVE sausages. It was hot and I had to let it cool a little. I would do anything for a warm sausage (except kiss a cat). I felt better already and moved closer to the fire to feel warmer.

'Ere, who 'as the tomato sauce?' enquired Murphy. They all laughed. Pat patted me on the head and tickled my ears.

'Where are you from then, little 'un? Where's your collar?'

'I'm lost,' I woofed but to Pat and the others it sounded like wooof.

'You'd better stay here and dry out, so. You can tell us your life story later,' chuckled Pat. They all laughed.

They let me take the best place by the fire. I lay with my tummy facing the heat which soon started to dry me out. I could see steam rising from my soggy fur and I started to feel warmer. The tramps talked amongst themselves, much of which I didn't understand. For example, they had a big discussion about a housing boom (but I hadn't heard any loud noises or explosions. I would know because I hate loud noises).

'I don't know where all the money is coming from,' puzzled Michael. 'When I was a boy on Inishmore[6] we didn't have two pennies to rub together. Still, I don't now, neither'.

'Aye, 'replied Pat, 'it's a great wonder. I expect it'll end in tears, so.'

'There'll be a popping and a crash,' added Michael, 'a great tinkling and fluttering as all the money crashes down.'

'At least there's c-c-casual work for the likes of us lads,' added Murphy, 'lap it up while you can.'

There was a murmur of agreement and they continued talking long into the night. They talked about how to find paid work, the best place to find food, the best places for begging, the Gardai, the weather, where to sleep and have a free shower, the best homeless shelters – 'it's the St Vincent for me, that's the best,' said Murphy – and so on. I started to feel tired and dozed off.

When I woke up it was morning and the tramps were tidying up their camp.

---

[6] The largest of the Arran Islands in the west of Ireland

'Murphy, put the brazier behind that bush until tonight,' commanded Pat. 'Com'on, young 'un, you'd better come with me. If the dog wardens catch you, you'll be taken to the pound and that'll be the end of you.'

I didn't know what Pat meant but I thought it would be best to stay with him. Maybe he could help me find my Keanes.

I trotted behind Pat all morning, hoping we might see Josie or Joe. I didn't recognise any of the places we went, and I started losing hope of ever seeing mum and the Keanes again. We ended up at a huge building with a glass roof, Pat called it Heuston Station. Even a dog like me, who normally has her nose to the ground sniffing, could not fail to notice what a huge place it was. I had never seen anything like it. It was so busy, not like the park. People were jostling, dodging and rushing about in all directions. Loud voices told people where to go to catch their train, sign boards with red lettering told people where the train went and what time it would leave and little shops and stalls sold drinks, snacks, newspapers and the like.

But Pat wasn't interested in taking a train; he went to check all the public phones for money. He found 60 cents in the return change trays, money rejected by the phones and left by the users, he explained. He put the money in the pocket of his long, brown coat. Then we walked over to the newspaper stand. Pat looked at the newspaper headlines.

'Always good to keep abreast of what's going on,' Pat told me. 'See, look here at this headline in the Dublin News – STRAY DOG CLAMPDOWN. Now that's worth knowing if you're a dog. You'll have to watch out, young 'un, you will, so.'

'Hey, you!' came a voice.

We turned around. A garda!

'Is that your dog?'

Without hesitation Pat replied. 'yes, Sor, it is, Sor.'

'If it's a stray it'll need to go to the pound,' replied the Garda.

'No, Sor, she's not a stray, she's my dog, so!' retorted Pat, stepping closer to me.

'Then what's its name?'

'She's called Tillie, Sor,' replied Pat, quick as a flash.

The Garda looked Pat up and down, he pursed his lips then scowled at me. I wondered who Tillie was.

'All right, move on!' he ordered, flicking his head towards the station exit.

Pat started to leave the station and I followed one step behind.

Just then a man wearing a red, stripy apron came out of a small supermarket opposite the station entrance and shouted, ''ere, he's the one that stole the sausages yesterday!'

The Garda, who had been walking away, turned around, saw the situation and looked at Pat. Pat shrugged and broke into a run down the street, crashing through the early crowd of commuters leaving the station. Before I knew it, I had lost sight of him. All I could see was a forest of legs, boots and shoes. I moved towards the wall of the building and picked up Pat's scent. Suddenly it was smothered by a strong perfume. I carried on going and picked it up again before losing it for good. I stopped and looked around. No sign of Pat. I ducked into an alley. I didn't want to be taken to the pound. I'd have to find the Keanes by myself. I started walking briskly back in the direction of the park, at least I thought it was the right direction. I hoped it was.

The sun was out now so it was feeling warmer. I walked and trotted and walked again but I just but couldn't seem to find the park. Eventually, when I was trudging miserably down a back alley, it started to rain again, spitting at first then heavily. I looked around for shelter and saw a covered entrance. It looked like a back door to a shop, but it was deep enough to keep me dry. Relieved, I crawled up the steps into the corner and curled up, watching the big rain drops splash and explode on the cobbles, before ganging together and spluttering down the gutter to the nearest drain.

After one day I was no better off. I was hungry, lost, damp and chilly. It had been a tiring day. While I was wondering what to do next, I must have fallen asleep.

Chapter 7 – Sinéad

A sudden sound woke me with a start. My head was up, ears alert. Silence. No, there it was again, a cat mewing. I poked my head out of the entrance. It was starting to become dark, but I could see the cat on top of a wheelie bin, mewing. It hadn't seen me. Maybe I've mentioned it before, but I love to chase cats – that's what cats are for, chasing!

I don't like cats. They hide in all sorts of places, under cars, on top of cars, in hedges, on shed roofs, curled up in flower tubs, in fact anywhere, so I have to keep my nose, eyes and ears on alert all the time. There are two types of cat

- The ones that run away when I chase them.
- Smarmy ones that sit on fences and cars, grinning stupidly, knowing I can't reach them.

The best way to find a cat is by following its scent. They smell of cat fur, ladies' perfume and cat food. Cats make me really excited. Anyway, this cat, mewing in the soppy way cats do and sitting on top of the wheelie bin in the alley, was no exception, just asking to be chased. It was one of those particularly haughty gingers, probably a stray as it was skinny with a bald patch on its rump. I ran at it. Despite my well developed hunting skills, it saw me coming and sprinted off down the alley, turning right. I ran after it, my rough paws skidding on the slippery, shiny cobbles of the wet alley as I turned the tight corner. The cat was escaping!

I saw it spring nimbly over a green wooden gate at the end of the alley. Still running, I followed and leapt at the gate. It was high but, at the speed I was going, I just managed to reach up with my front paws and haul myself over the top, aided by a push from my back legs on a bar across the gate. I landed and looked around, a walled garden, lots of shrubs, no sign of ginger.

'Where are you, ginger? Come on, let's play,' I woofed.

A rustle in the bush above and something moving on my right caught my attention. Ginger was in the bush and, just as I caught sight of it, it stepped onto the high garden wall, stopped and looked down at me in that haughty way cats have. Grrrr!

I barked at it until it trotted off along the wall. Once its tail had disappeared, I decided to check out where I was. I was in a long, high walled garden with a tall, narrow three-story house at the far end. On my right were the bushes, some starting to blossom with big red flowers. They filled the air with sweet scent. On my left was a large shed, with peeling paint and a slight lean, and beyond this some flower beds. In front of me was a tidy lawn, neatly mowed with carefully cut edges.

I thought I ought to go so I went back to vault over the gate. I tried and failed. I tried again, it was too high. But wait a minute, I thought, I came this way so I must be able to jump it. I was running when chasing ginger and I cleared the gate that time. Maybe I should run as I jumped at the gate? I trotted back into the garden, turned around and ran, propelling myself up with a huge leap and, smack, my head hit the top of the gate and I fell back, stunned. I lay dazed, looking out into the alley. Then I realised that the alley was quite a bit higher than the garden path I was on, there was a step up to the alley, so I needed to jump higher from inside than I did from outside. I sat down again to think what this meant. Was I trapped?

As I was here, I thought, I may as well have a sniff around, so I did. I could smell cats, two, and people. The people smell was strong near some chairs on the patio and by the doors into the house. A light shone from the doors, French windows they are called, though they are in fact doors. I looked inside and jumped in fright!

Looking back at me, from inside the house, was a girl, a teenage girl, kneeling on all fours. She had long blond hair and steely grey eyes that bored into you. She tapped on the window and said something I couldn't hear.

I froze, still as a rock. I looked at her.

She looked at me.

She tapped on the window again. Again she spoke.

I wagged my tail. It seemed a sensible thing to do. She reached up and opened the door.

'I said, what *are* you doing in my garden?' she asked, stooping down.

I wagged my tail again. It still seemed the sensible thing to do.

The girl looked behind her.

'Are you hungry?'

Well if you know anything about dogs you know that's a bit of a silly question. Dogs never refuse food, at least Izzie dogs never do.

'Wait here' she said quickly, closing the door and disappearing into the house.

I waited.

Soon she came back with a saucer of cold chicken bits. She opened the door and stepped outside, putting the saucer down on the patio. Then she sat on a patio chair.

'Go on,' she ordered, pointing to the saucer, 'eat up! Quick, in case my dad comes back.'

I started eating.

Yum!

Yum!

Gone.

'He probably won't come back until much later, though,' she continued. 'He's busy working. He's always working, ever since mum died and he has to run the business on his own. I don't suppose you know what a business is, do you, after all you're just a furry dog? Anyway, he hardly knows I'm here. Oh, you've finished. That was quick! He won't let me have a dog, says they take too much time. Maybe I could adopt you. No, Dad wouldn't let me. Who do you belong to anyway? Oh, are you thirsty? Hang on!'

She picked up the saucer and took it over to a tap on the wall, filling it to the brim with water.

'Here you go, I expect you're thirsty. I know what it's like. Gogs, that's Mrs Goggins the housekeeper, always puts too much salt on the food. I keep telling her it's not healthy but she's very set in her ways so I'm always drinking. She's *reeeaaally* old. I mean ancient, probably pre-historic, I expect she knew all the dinosaurs by their first names. Used to be dad's nanny and she came to help when, well you know, when mum....'

She tailed off and paused for breath. I licked her hand consolingly. I wondered if this girl ever stopped talking.

'Anyway, where *have* you come from? And where's your collar?' she asked.

She looked at me with her steely grey eyes, then stood up and strolled down the garden towards the gate.

'Come on,' she turned and gestured, 'back home for you.' She opened the gate, standing to one side to let me pass.

I hesitated, I had nowhere to go. I wagged my tail.

'Go on, 'she commanded, 'you can't stay here!'

I moved slowly towards the gate using my slow-motion walk. This is the walk I use when I don't want to do what I'm told. It's so slow a tortoise would overtake me. There was nothing out there for me. 'Home' was an empty doorway in an alleyway. I hesitated again. On my right was the garden shed. I saw it had a large hole where the bottom of a plank had rotted or broken off. It looked more inviting than my doorway. I made a dash for it and before the girl could say anything I was through the hole and inside the shed.

It was gloomy and I bumped my head on a metal bucket. It smelt of soil, chemicals and mice but it was warm and dry, and suddenly much brighter. The girl had opened the door.

'What are you doing?' she asked crossly. 'Haven't you a home to go to?'

She paused, looking at me, 'maybe you haven't. Hmmm, you haven't, have you? Are you lost? Or maybe a stray?'

I sat down, then I lay on my back so she could rub my tummy.

'Don't do that, you'll make your fur all dirty. Oh, I suppose you could stay here for a bit. I'll bring you some breakfast in the morning. Here, you can make your bed on this old chair cushion. I know it's a bit tatty, but it'll do for now. I 'll fetch a saucer of water for you.'

She disappeared only to immediately stick her head around the door.

'By the way, I 'm Sinéad. What's your name? Only joking, I know a dog can't talk!'

'Izzie,' I woofed.

'OK, I'll call you Woofie.'

She disappeared again and I settled down on the cushion.

Sinéad returned with the saucer and put it down by my bed. Then she stroked my head.

'I'll shut the door. If you need to go out, use the hole. Oh, and don't poop on the grass. Gogs will go mad, do it in the bushes. See you tomorrow.'

With that she was gone, the door shut. I was alone again, but at least now I had a friend.

I explored the shed, it wasn't big. Although I could smell mice, there weren't any in the shed, maybe they had wintered there and left now the weather was warmer. The window and corners of the shed were covered in cobwebs. One or two spiders scuttled about. A small fly, caught in a web, buzzed frantically. There were garden tools hanging on the walls and piled up in a corner next to a grubby old bucket, bags of pongy chemicals and some chairs. Nothing of interest to a stray dog.

I curled up, content to be fed and glad of a dry, warm place to sleep. I couldn't help thinking what I should do next. Maybe Sinéad would realise I'm lost and find my Keanes. The thought was so exciting it took me a long time to fall asleep.

Chapter 8 – New Hope

I awoke to a bright and sunny morning. The sunshine shone through the shed window and between some cracks, making a dappled effect of shifting patterns inside the shed, as the tall bushes outside swayed gently in a light breeze and filtered the rays. My bed was comfortable, but I needed to stand up and stretch. I squeezed through the hole into the garden, green and brightly lit, peaceful except for the bird's dawn chorus and the odd rustle of leaves in the breeze. I sniffed around for scents - cats, Sinéad, lavender bushes. I explored for some time, then went over to the French window. I looked in. No sign of Sinéad. I lay down in the sun to wait.

After a while, the door opened. Sinéad's head popped out.

'Woofie! What are you doing? You're meant to be in the shed!'

I wagged my tail and turned on my back so she could stroke my tummy. I find this is always a good idea when I 'm in trouble.

'Oooh, wait there, then,' she added and was gone.

A minute later and she was back with a saucerful of cold lamb and broken biscuit. A strange combination you may think but, to a dog with a rumbly tummy, it's yummy. I ate it quickly and looked at Sinéad.

'Can we go for a hunt now?' I woofed.

'Sinéad,' came a voice from inside the house, 'do you want a packed lunch for school today?'

'Yes, please, Mrs Goggins,' Sinéad called back. She lowered her voice, 'I have to go now Woofie, but I 'll see you tonight. Keep out of sight, best to stay in the shed. Bye.'

With that she went back into the house, closed the door, put the empty saucer under a sofa, turned and gave me a wave and a shoo motion.

I trotted off back to the shed, where I settled down on my bed and started to wash and groom myself. Grooming is important to a dog like me. I wondered when Sinéad would be back.

I must have dozed for a while. When I awoke it was even sunnier so I thought I would go out and stretch my legs around the garden. I squeezed through the hole and decided to investigate the bushes more closely. This was fun as they were quite dense and there were a number of new smells. Tiring of this I decided to explore the rest of the garden, enjoying the warm sun on my fur. As I stepped onto the patio, the stones felt warm to my paws. I lay down for a sunbathe. Lovely! This is what a dog's life is all about, I thought.

Suddenly I heard the French window open. I twisted round and saw someone who wasn't Sinéad. I darted into the nearest bush and crept along the edge of the garden wall towards the shed. I paused behind a particularly thick bush and peered out. A gray-haired lady was standing with her back to me, hanging clothes on a line. I darted across the grass and through the hole in the shed. I hoped I hadn't been seen. I waited, hiding behind the metal bucket.

After a short time, I heard the French windows close. I realised I would have to be careful going out into the garden.

The rest of the day I spent resting in he shed and having the odd walk in the garden, under cover of the bushes. Towards the end of the afternoon I heard footsteps coming across the grass and the shed door opened. It was Sinéad. I wagged my tail.

'Wooaf,' I woofed, meaning hi, nice to see you.

'It's OK, Woofie, Gogs has gone shopping and she'll be ages, always is and Dad's at work. Look, I've brought you some Shreddies as we don't have dog biscuits. I checked about feeding dogs on the internet, two meals a day plus snacks, so I stopped by the corner shop and bought two tins of dog food. It says on the tin that dogs love it. I hope you like it.'

She took two tins of dog food out of her satchel to show me.

'Woo-oohf,' I woofed, meaning that looks tasty, thanks.

'You can have it later,' she said putting the tins to one side, 'I've been thinking what to do. I would like to keep you but Dad won't approve, assuming he notices that is!' Sinéad raised her eyes to the sky in a dismissive gesture. 'We should advertise really. I could take your photo and put it in the paper. That way your owners will see you. Well, hopefully,' she added.

'What do you think? Anyway, you can't stay in this shed forever, can you?'

I wagged my tail, I liked Sinéad but I did want to try to find mum and the Keanes.

'Right, that's agreed. I'll talk to Dad at breakfast and get it sorted. I'll be back later with a tin opener for your dinner.'

She knelt beside me and stroked the top of my head.

'Gosh, your fur is so soft, Woofie, I could stroke it all day,' she murmured, 'I wish I could keep you.'

I licked her nose. She laughed then stood up to go.

'See you later, when I've done my homework,'

She shut the door and was gone.

Later that evening Sinéad came back with the promised tin opener. She read the tin label carefully, then opened the tin. She stopped.

'Oh, by the way, good news,' she chirped, 'dad was home early. He closed a big deal today and he's as pleased as Punch, so I mentioned you. He thought it was a good idea to advertise in the Dublin People and the Dublin News, and he doesn't mind you staying in the shed and garden until we find your owner. I 'll tell

Gogs tomorrow. She's away tonight at her sister's but she'll be back in the morning. Now, let me take your photo. Did I tell you I want to be a professional photographer? My art teacher says I have a talent, just like my mum. Come on, outside in the sun, I have the camera.'

We went into the garden.

'Sit there in the sunshine, yes, there.'

I sat looking at Sinéad. I wasn't clear what she was trying to do but I trusted her.

'You look just like a grey, furry blob, it's really hard to make you out or what size you are or anything. I know,' she went to the edge of the patio and picked up a colourful statue of a funny little man, about as tall as me.

'If I put this garden gnome next to you, it will give people some idea of your size.'

I wasn't sure about being photographed next to a gnome. I gave it a good sniff and it smelt harmless enough, so I thought I ought to oblige, after all Sinéad was trying to help me.

'OK, smile, Woofie. Are you smiling? I can't tell. OK, here goes, ready, stop washing and look at me, say

'Sausages' ' – my ears pricked up and she had my full attention – Flash, click.

Sinéad looked at the camera.

'It'll do, hmmmm, maybe I'll be a professional animal photographer when I leave school, that sounds like fun.'

She sat on the grass and pulled a piece of paper out of her pocket.

'I've drafted the advert, listen.

Found in Arbour Hill area, small, grey, furry dog (female), friendly, no collar, white patch on chest. Owner contact Sinéad at...

and then our house phone number, Dad told me not to use my mobile.'

Sinéad sat and chatted to me for a while. Keeping close, I sat next to her and listened. She told me about her mum, who had died last year after a short illness, about her hard-working Dad and Mrs Goggins. She told me about her friends at school and how they had helped her through a difficult year, and her best friend, Aoife, who was like a sister to her (not the sort you hate and argue with all the time but the sort you swopped clothes and went shopping with). She told me about her plans to be a photographer. She told me about so many things. I didn't understand everything, but I sat and listened politely, with my ears pricked up and my head to one side. It's amazing what people tell their pets.

'You're a good listener, Woofie. Thanks. Well, I'd better go and upload this advert on the websites.'

Sinéad stood up and turned to go.

I barked and jumped up at her. I gave my 'I'm hungry' woof.

Sinéad turned back.

'What is it, Woofie? Of course, you want your dinner, is that it?' I wagged my tail extra hard. 'Come on, then.'

We went back to the shed and Sinéad spooned out a half tin.

'See you tomorrow.'

And then she was gone, and I was on my own again. I ate my dinner then, as the shadows started to disappear and the darkness descended, I sat thinking about what tomorrow would bring and whether Joe and Josie would see the advert.

Chapter 9 – More Trouble

I awoke from a dream about chasing squirrels with mum in the park. I was excited about Sinéad finding my mum and the Keanes. I went outside to stretch and sniff about in the early morning sunshine. I watched a robin peck around in the flowerbed and take little grubs to its nest to feed its young. After a while I lay down by the French Window to wait for Sinéad. Soon the door clicked open and out she stepped. She tickled me behind the ears.

'Morning, Woofie. The adverts will be in both papers tonight. You owe me eight Euro, only kidding, Dad paid, at least his credit card did. Hopefully we'll hear something tonight or tomorrow. Come on, let's get your breakfast.'

We went to the shed, where Sinéad gave me my breakfast. You may be thinking that a lot of this story is about eating but, after all, I'm a dog and that's what we think about a lot. That and going for a hunt and chasing things. Anyway, Sinéad told me her plans for the day. Double maths (ugh!), double art (hooray!), lunch with Aoife and their friends at the local café (probably a cheese and pesto panini) followed by French (OK, mais oui!) and PE (always good for a laugh). She explained that she had considered putting me in her bag and taking me to school, but had decided I might not fit and I might be bored at school. Instead she would bring Aoife back home to meet me after school. Aoife liked animals, especially furry ones. She wanted to be a vet. I was to be on my best behaviour. With that she left for school.

I lay in the sun awhile and dozed. Then I chased a few sparrows and blackbirds around the garden, just for fun and for the exercise.

Around midday, I heard the French window open. I sat up and turned around. It was the grey-haired woman, presumably Mrs Goggins. She saw me and stopped in her tracks.

'What are you doing here!' she demanded, waving her hand at me, 'go on shoo, out, shoo.'

I wagged my tail.

'Don't you wag you tail at me, you don't belong here. How did you get in? Go on, shoo!'

She walked down the garden and opened the back gate, standing to one side.

'Out, go on, shoo.'

I wagged my tail and woo-wooaafed to tell her that Sinéad was looking after me and it was OK for me to stay in the garden.

'Right, I'll sort you out.'

She went back into the house and came out with a broom, which she used to push me towards the gate. I turned, darted towards the shed and went through the hole.

It went quiet.......

I could hear Mrs Goggin moving about in the garden. Maybe Sinéad would be home soon.

Suddenly, the shed door opened and there was Mrs Goggins, silhouetted in the doorframe. The next thing I knew I was under a deluge of water from a garden hose. I hate being wet (except when paddling and chasing ducks through the water) so I nipped through the hole out into the garden and paused to shake myself dry.

More water hit me full in the face followed by the brush in the midriff. Before I knew it, I was in the alley and the gate was slammed in my face.

I sat there stunned. I shook myself. I was soaking, like a soggy sponge.

Mrs Goggins stood looking over the gate.

'Go on now, shoo,' and with that she walked off back to the house.

I sat there, dripping and bruised, collecting my thoughts.

I realised I would have to wait at the gate for Sinéad to come home and find me, so that's what I did.

The morning drew on and there was no sign of Mrs Goggins. The day was becoming warm and the sun moved around until the alley was in full sunshine and I started to dry out. I began to feel peckish so I thought I could wander up and down the alley a little way to see if I could find any food. I had been looking for a little while without luck, when I heard a swishing, whirring noise at the end of the alley. I looked towards it and could see a small vehicle moving towards me. It had a white body with glass at the front, below which were two blue brushes whirring away, sweeping up the rubbish.

I hesitated nervously. It looked like a giant hoover and it kept coming towards me. I turned and retreated down the alley, taking a few steps before looking back.

It was still swishing and whirring towards me, and it was closer.

I moved away some more.

It continued crawling its way down the alley.

I sped off down the alley and turned the corner. I peeked around the wall.

It was still creeping along, unstoppable.

I backed away and before I knew it, the big hoover had turned the corner and was coming straight at me.

I scarpered. I passed a couple of alleys then dodged right into another. The hoover's sound became quieter but started to sound louder again once I stopped. I peeked around the corner. It was still coming in my direction. I turned and ran down the alley, left, right, straight on, until I could hear the hoover moving on in the distance. The noise was quieter now, so I knew it must be going away. I started to retrace my steps back to Sinéad's gate. I came to her alley and walked up to her gate, at least where her gate should have been but wasn't. I went a bit further then retraced my steps. I looked up and down. It looked like Sinéad's alley, but it clearly wasn't. I was lost again!

I sat down to think.

Aha, I thought, all I have to do is try the next alley and if that isn't right the one after that. I can't have travelled very far. I just had to keep looking. Maybe I could pick up my scent, assuming the hoover hadn't removed it.

Suddenly, I came across the open gate as I was walking down the next alley. I poked my head inside and there were two bowls of dog food. You may recall, dear reader, that I started the book with this little episode so now I will finish it. I was hungry so decided to nibble some of the food. That's when Bull and Cumberland turned up, my mouth in their dinner and their dinner in my mouth.

Bull came around the corner first. He stopped and glared at me in a way only bull terriers can. Then he looked at the bowl. Unconsciously, I licked my lips. Oops. Tasty but trouble, I thought.

'Wadya doin', kid? That's Cumberland's dinner,' he growled, 'Cumberland, come 'ere!'

Cumberland trotted out from behind him - fat, round, brown and all sausage dog, ears almost sweeping the ground.

''E's eating your dinner, Cumberland, 'e is.'

Cumberland growled and moved to my left, while Bull started to move around to my right. I apologised and ran. I thought I had got away with it, but they chased me down the street and into the alley that led to the park. In the alley, my way was barred by the big iron gates, both shut. I was trapped.

I turned to face Bull. Cumberland was nowhere in sight.

'Hey, I'm sorry, let's talk about this,' I suggested.

'When I've bitten you to bits,' snarled Bull, showing his teeth up to the gums.

Just then Cumberland came running around the corner, panting. Slowing, catching his breath, his stomach wobbling from side to side, he walked up beside Bull. They started walking towards me, menacingly. Bull bared his brown teeth and gave me a snarlie. I backed away slowly until my back was up against the gates.

Suddenly, from a house on my left there was a big commotion, barking and meowing. A tabby cat shot out of a cat flap followed by the head of a big dog which barked and disappeared as quickly as it had appeared. Tabby flew straight into Cumberland, crashing into him as the two rolled over and over, all tangled up together, a brown, stripy, furry ball of ears, legs, paws, tails and claws.   Tabby was the first to jump up and head for the gate, nimbly nipping between the bars.   Now, you might not know this, but sausage dogs have the brains of a biscuit and Cumberland followed at speed, clearly not seeing the danger ahead. His head and shoulders went through the bars but the rest of him didn't.   He was stuck.   Tabby turned and meowed in his face.   Cumberland was barking like mad and wriggling and struggling to squeeze through.   Bull forgot all about me and went to help Cumberland.

I had the presence of mind to scarper.   I ran back down the alley into the street and dodged in and out of the people.   I turned left and right, then left again. After a few minutes I stopped to catch my breath, listening for sounds of a pursuit over my laboured breathing.   I heard traffic and people but no dogs.

I was exhausted and it had started to rain again. The alleyway where I stopped was quiet so I thought I would be safe for a while.   I had no idea where I was but at least I knew I was near the park again.   I would set out in the morning to find a way into the park, maybe I could find my own way home.   In the meantime, I needed a place to curl up and recover. I looked around.

On my left was a pile of boxes, one of which, a wooden crate, was on its side and empty. I crawled inside to rest and keep dry. I must have dozed off dreaming about the park.

Chapter 10 – Benni

I first met Benni in the rain. It was still tipping it down and, as I hate rain, I was still sheltering inside the wooden crate when he came running up and dived in next to me. He didn't see me until he bumped into me.

'Oops,' he grunted, 'mind if we share the box?' He shook himself, spraying me with water as he did so.

'OK,' I replied, not minding some company, and really not having much choice as Benni had squeezed in and made himself at home. The new arrival was the same colour as me and smelt doggy damp, even more doggy damp than I did. I looked at him, nose to tail. I sniffed him all over.

'What sort of dog are you?' I asked.

'A Schnauzer.'

'Bless you! You're wet through,' I exclaimed.

'I didn't sneeze! I said I was a Schnauzer.'

'Oh.' I thought and replied, 'I'm an Izzie.'

'An Izzie? What sort of dog is an Izzie?' inquired the new arrival, looking me up and down.

'A dog like me,' I replied defensively.

'Oh well, nice to meet you. My name's Benni.'

'I thought you were Schnauzer?' queried Izzie.

'I am. A Schnauzer called Benni.'

'Then I must be an Izzie called Izzie.'

Benni looked at me out of the corner of one eye and raised an eyebrow. 'If you say so, kid, but you look more like a terrier to me, bit of Kerry Blue maybe.'

A terrier with a bit of Kerry Blue, I thought, I had heard those words used when Ma Keane had been describing my siblings to the people who bought them. I knew mum was a Kerry Blue.

'What's a terrier, Benni?' I asked.

'A type of dog. I'm a Schnauzer, you're a terrier. At least you look like a terrier. Terriers chase things, like squirrels and cats.'

'You're right, I must be a terrier, I often chase those sorts of animals,' I replied excitedly, reminding myself that they often lead me into trouble. No doubt about it, I thought, a terrier, with a bit of Kerry Blue!

He shook again, covering me with a fine spray of water. I gave a little growl, because I hate being wet, but at least it was still drier under the box.

'What are you doing here anyway, kid?' queried Benni, shifting onto his side so he faced me.

I explained I was lost, told him all about my recent problems and how I was hoping to find the park again so I could find my Keanes and mum.

'Wow, some adventure, kid. I might be able to help. Let's see later. When it's stopped pouring down.'

We sat and watched the rain for a while. Big drops spattered on the cobbles, bouncing back up in a cascade of little drops, before falling back to the ground. The water ran down the gutters and away to a nearby drain, which gurgled it down thirstily. The box was on a slight rise so we stayed dry. It was nice to have Benni's warmth next to me. Benni dozed a bit. He was bigger than me, had floppy, pointy ears and, like me, was grey, although he had white socks and white around the mouth. Maybe he's been eating cream I thought but, when I looked more closely, I realised it was just white fur like on his legs. His fur was long and I could see he had been on the street for a while.

He was cute but, best of all, I liked his long, feathery eyelashes.

After a while Benni sat up and turned to me.

'When this torrent stops I'm off to the chip shop for supper. Want to come?'

I wasn't sure what a chip shop was but, as I was really hungry and supper was mentioned, I thought it must be a good place to go and I would tag along. The rain was starting to ease but the light was fading.

'Where are you from, Benni?' I asked.

'Nowhere. Or at least I can't remember. I've been on the streets for a year or two, since I was little. I've had to learn the hard way.'

I could learn a lot from Benni, I thought, a little sad about the idea that I might be roaming the streets for years. In that case, I thought to myself, I'd better learn fast. But would Benni help me?

I looked at Benni. He was looking up and down the alley, still from the safety of the box.

'Benni,' I started, 'will you teach me what you know? Can I hang out with you, you know, for a bit, until I find my mum again?'

Benni, who had returned to resting his head on his paws with his eyes shut, opened one shiny eye and looked at me. He paused while he considered.

'Sure, kid, I like you. I'll teach you the Way – the Street Way - but first some rules. One, I'm top dog, OK?'

'Sure, you're top dog.'

'Two, I lead when scavenging for food and I have first choice of what we find.'

'OK.'

'Three, when in public make out like you're with people, not a stray.'

'Right,' I agreed, thinking that's probably not as easy as it sounds.

'Four, if you see the dog warden's yellow van, run, it's every dog for himself.'

'Oh, er, OK. What's a dog warden, Benni?'

'They catch stray dogs like us and take them away.'

'Where would they take us?' I queried.

'Who knows, nowhere good I expect. I've never seen a dog again after the Wardens take it away. Just watch out for yellow vans,' Benni reminded me.

'Right, it's stopped raining. Let's go and nosh on some fish and chips.'

Benni stood up and trotted down the alley, with me at his heels, tail in the air. Turning left into another alley brought new smells of fish, chicken, sausages and chips. My mouth was watering already. Benni stopped and turned to me.

'Hey, kid, do you know how to make doggy eyes?'

I was a little puzzled by this question, as I thought all dogs were born with all the eyes they needed. I suppose I looked a bit blank so Benni continued.

'You know, how to look doggy sad. Listen, first look at the person with the food, cock your head a little to the right, or left, and open your eyes wide. If you are not given something straight away, look glumly at the ground, whimper then gaze wistfully at the person. It usually works.'

'OK, I can do that.'

'Right, let's go. And remember, look like you belong.'

We turned the corner and surveyed the scene. There was a group of young people eating fish and chips near the chip shop entrance. We went closer (not too close whispered Benni, they can kick), sat down and started making doggy eyes. I chose a young girl in a short skirt and Benni chose a young man in jeans.

'Ah, will you look here,' purred the girl, 'what a lovely little dog,' as she bent down to say hello.

'Watch it, it may bite,' warned one of the young men. To show that I wouldn't bite, I lay down on my back so she could stroke my tummy.

'Neat trick, kid,' whispered Benni, clearly impressed.

'Have a chip, little one,' she said, throwing me a huge chip. I twisted, caught it in mid air and wolfed it down.

'Clever dog. Go on, Mick, give the other one a chip.' Mick threw Benni a chip which he caught in mid-air too.

'Come on,' said the girl, 'let's go to the park.'

Park! That's where I wanted to go. Maybe I would find Josie or Joe. I was about to follow them but Benni thought it wasn't a good idea. If people feel pestered, they might become cross and then there'll be trouble, he told me. Anyway, the light was started to fade so we had to be careful.

So, we sat outside the chip shop, looking like we belonged, making doggy eyes and being fed chips and once a piece of sausage. After a while we were full and decided to go back to our box for the night.

Over the next few days Benni taught me a lot about living on the street, about how to scavenge for food, how to look like I belonged to a person, that sort of thing. We would go around to the back of restaurants that Benni had visited before. Usually the chefs knew Benni and were friendly, so we were given a few scraps when they came out for some fresh air or a smoke, or both.

'Hello,' said one lady chef at a Chinese restaurant, 'you've got a friend today. Come here little one.'

I walked forward slowly and carefully, she held out her hand for me to sniff then patted me on the head.

'No collar? Are you lost too? Here, have this duck a l'orange the big, elderly gentleman in the window didn't want.'

Benni and I tucked into the duck. It was delicious! I had never tasted anything so good. I couldn't stop licking my lips and nose for ages afterwards.

'You know, kid,' Benni said to me afterwards, as we left, 'you're good at this scavenging. We make a good team.'

As we trotted back to our box, we passed the front of the shop and we saw the elderly man eating a huge ice cream. Maybe tomorrow we could have some ice cream. I was feeling really pleased with myself and still licking my lips as we turned the corner into our alley.

'Uh oh,' Benni groaned, stopping in his tracks.

'What is it, Benni?' then I saw. Our box had gone.

Chapter 11 – Adventures in the park

With our box gone we had to find somewhere else to shelter for the night. I was worried and must have looked it.

'Don't worry, kid,' said Benni protectively, 'I'll look after you. Let's go to the park.'

The park, Phoenix Park I was to discover, is the largest urban park in Europe. To a little dog like me it is HUGE. I think it was probably the same park where I became lost, but it was so big it could have been a different place.

Benni and I made a cosy, homely den in the bushes by an old wall. Large walls on two sides, some bushes and a huge fir tree kept the den dry and hidden. We had to crawl around a pile of leaves and under a bush to squeeze in, so it was really hard to see us from outside. A few days later Benni found an old, pink baby's blanket in the park and dragged it in for us to lie on.

It was a brilliant spot because we were near a fast food kiosk and in the late evening, after the girl running the kiosk had gone home, and in the early morning, we went scavenging for dropped food. There was usually enough. People are so careless and wasteful with their food, luckily for us dogs! I expect the kiosk owner wondered why the area was so clean when she came back in the morning to open up. Of course, we couldn't clear up the litter people left. That was a real nuisance for us animals. Once I saw a squirrel with a plastic ring stuck round its body. It must have become caught in the plastic whilst scavenging, poor thing.

Our den faced west so after a successful evening scavenging, we would lie and watch the sun go down, slowly sinking behind the tall monument that pointed to the sky and had lots of steps[7], silhouetted by the orange sunset behind it. Sometimes, on fine nights, we would listen to the park become quiet. As it grew dark and the noise of the traffic reduced, we could hear the sounds of nearby Dublin Zoo. We liked to watch the

---

[7] Izzie probably means the Wellington Monument in Phoenix Park

stars come out. Benni recalled his owner who had liked stargazing, so he knew a bit about stars.

'He was always taking his girlfriends out to show them the stars,' he explained. 'Maybe that's why he had so many!' he added.

'I love the stars, I love the twinkles,' I replied.

'I learnt a bit about them. That's the moon, over there just above the church steeple.'

'It's huge! Where has it come from?' I asked.

'It just goes round and round the Earth every few weeks, and it's lit up by sunshine, which is amazing really as it's nighttime now,' Benni replied knowledgably but a little uncertainly. 'And that star over there, the bright one, is Sirius, also called the Dog Star.'

'Wow, I didn't know dogs lived in space, that's amazing. Maybe we could be astrodogs and fly there.'

'I don't think so, Izzie, but we can make Sirius our star if you like.'

'What a great idea, Benni, I've never had a star before.'

Often, as it could still be chilly at night, we would curl up together on our blanket to keep warm, a pile of scavenged food at our side. Benni would tell me a story about Mickey Mouse and Pluto, his dog.

'You see, Izzie, Mickey Mouse wanted to go to the Moon so he decided he would build a huge pile of boxes and climb up to the top to reach it. So, he and Pluto searched all around the neighbourhood looking for old boxes, wooden ones, cardboard ones, old crates, anything. When they looked at the big pile they had collected Mickey thought they would need more, so they knocked on all the doors and asked in all the shops and offices and collected even more boxes. Then Mickey started building a huge tower of boxes, one on top of another. As it approached the moon, the tower started to wobble and sway a bit but luckily it wasn't a windy night. Soon Mickey was nearly there and realised he just needed one more box to reach the Moon.'

'What did he do, Benni?'

'He called down to Pluto to say he needed one more box and could Pluto tie one to the piece of string he was dangling down. So, Pluto looked around but there wasn't a single box to be found, not even a shoe box or a match box. By now Mickey was getting impatient, the moon was so close, but the tower was swaying quite a bit. He called down to Pluto to hurry up. 'Come on you dippy dog,' he called, 'hurry up!'. I know, thought Pluto, scratching his head and now in a bit of a fluster, I'll take the box from the bottom of the pile and pass it up. So he did.'

'Oh,' I said thoughtfully, 'but if he did that............ooooh.....'

Benni nodded and we would have a laugh before dozing off in the safety of our den.

In the morning, when the sun was coming up again and after snacking at the kiosk, I would go and chase the ducks or squirrels around the park. Not only was this good fun, it also warmed me up after a chilly sleep. Sometimes I was so excited about chasing the ducks that I would jump in the water after them as they tried to escape, but I never caught any. The squirrels would always run up the nearest tree, which I thought was unfair but pretty clever really, because they know dogs can't climb trees. At least it gave me a good run around and a bit of exercise. Sometimes Benni would join in but usually he would just trot along with me and keep me in sight. If I couldn't see him I would stop, look around and, if he wasn't there, go back and find him before running off again.

One day I was lying under the fast food kiosk, watching people sitting in the sun and eating their burgers and chips, pretending to belong to the girl running the kiosk, when I saw the greyhound that had chased me into the bushes the day I became lost. I started to growl to myself. Should I bark at it or, maybe I thought, I could ask it where we were when we collided, so I could find the part of the park that Josie and Joe played in. I watched it prance past, looking superior and thought, what did have I to lose?

I shuffled out from under the kiosk.

'Excuse me, greyhound, do you remember me?' I asked politely.

It turned and looked down at me, literally and metaphorically[8]

'You! I remember chasing you. Do you want me to do it again, kid?'

'No, thank you,' I replied respectfully, ambling along beside it and noting it was on a lead anyway. 'I did say I was sorry for knocking you down and I was

---

[8] Literally because the greyhound was taller than Izzie and metaphorically because the greyhound considered itself a superior being to a fluffy little mixed breed terrier.

hoping you could tell me where we were when I bumped into you that day.'

The greyhound looked down at me, as did its owner. who now realised I was following them.

'Get lost, runt, or I'll chase you again,' it sneered as only a greyhound can sneer.

'No, you won't, you're on a lead, peanut brain,' I quipped back.

It turned and growled at me so I gave it a few of my best aggressive barks. That shook it, I can tell you. It recoiled and then its owner pulled the lead and dragged it away and told me to get lost too! If only he knew that I was already lost! I couldn't help having a little laugh to myself as I trotted back to the kiosk to tell Benni what had happened.

The weather was becoming warmer and people started to eat their lunches in the park. Smartly dressed men and women sat on the benches, or sometimes on the ground or under trees in the shade, nibbling sandwiches and crisps from packets. Some talked quietly and sat close to each other. Others were noisy, laughing and joking. At weekends, families came for picnics.

These people would often provide us with lunch. We would trot up to them and sit nearby so we looked, to others, like their dog, not a stray. Eventually most would talk to us and offer us food, especially as they came to know us well.

Our favourite was a family of four who came at weekends. They came every Saturday even if the Sun wasn't shining and sat under al old oak tree. They did it properly. Rug on the ground, hamper, the lot. We were cautious at the beginning. Benni and I approached them purposely, not too close though, and lay down with our head on our front paws. We just looked at them with doggy eyes. The children saw us first.

'Mum, can we give the dogs a crisp?' asked the little blond girl with ponytails and a pink ribbon.

'I don't think you should encourage them, Gail. Their owners might not like us feeding them or they could be strays,' her mum replied, as she handed out the sandwiches and crisps.

I raised by ears, tilted my head to one side and looked as sad as I could. I gave a little whine.

'Go on, mum,' the tubby boy moaned. 'They look hungry and the little, fluffy grey one is so cute!'

'Go on, just one' the man said.

'Really, John, don't encourage them,' snapped the woman.

John shrugged, 'it'll do no harm.'

The little girl threw me a crisp. Luckily it was plain as I'm fussy about crisp flavours. Of course, I would thankfully have eaten any flavour then. The boy threw one to Benni.

Both crisps disappeared promptly. We continued lying quietly in the sunshine, making doggy eyes.

'Mum, I can't eat all my sandwich. Can the dogs have it?' asked Gail.

'They may as well if you're going to waste it,' came the cross reply.

She threw half a cheese sandwich towards us. We took a couple of bites each.

'Look, they're sharing it!' exclaimed Gail, 'maybe they're brother and sister too!'

'Don't be silly!' chuckled Tubby, 'they don't look anything like each other.'

'They do too, they're both grey for starters,' Gail retorted.

'Come on, you two,' ordered the man, 'we're off home, help tidy up and put this stuff away.'

And that was the end of that picnic.

The next weekend they were there again. Benni and I sidled up and sat down, looking cute. This time Gail came up to us, a little warily.

'I made you both a cheese sandwich, as I know you like cheese,' she whispered, giving us a huge sandwich. Benni took it gingerly and I licked Gail's hand to say thank you.

'Ooh, it licked my hand!' she exclaimed, pulling her hand away in surprise.

'Gail, come away, they might have fleas or something.'

'Yes, mum.'

'Wipe your hand with this and eat your sandwich!'

'Yes, mum.'

Well, over time the mum realised we were sociable, well behaved dogs and didn't have fleas, although we were a bit scruffy. We became regular visitors to their picnic and Gail always brought us a big cheese sandwich to share. Similar tactics worked on the people who had lunch in the park during the week. Most people were kind and generous and we made friends with all sorts of people who gave us scraps. I used to look out for my mum, Josie and Joe or Ma or Pa Keane, but I never saw them. It was a large park so maybe that's not surprising.

One day we saw an enormous lady on a bench. The buttons on her bulging blue blouse were nearly popping off. She was so bulky she took up half the bench. Benni and I looked at each other.

'Are you thinking what I'm thinking?' asked Benni.

'Fat lady, lots of food?' I replied.

'Exactly, come on.'

We sidled up to her and made doggy eyes until she noticed us.

'What do you two fleabags want? Shoo, go on, shoo,' she shouted waving her arm at us and wobbling all over as she did so.

Benni and I looked at each other but stood our ground, hoping she might change her mind and, to be honest, partly influenced by the huge bag of food she had next to her on the bench.

'You're strays, I hate strays, you should all be rounded up and shot, you horrible fleabags. I know,' she muttered, pulling out her mobile phone from her bag, 'I'll call the dog wardens!'

'Come on Izzie, time to make ourselves scarce,' said Benni, as the fat lady started talking into her phone.

Chapter 12 – A Sausage too Far

Early next morning I lay awake, listening to the sounds of the park. We had lived there for four or five weeks and it felt like home. It was one of those days when the scent of dawn filled the air, as the plants started to wake up in the warm sunshine, which filtered and rippled its way through the leaves of the trees and danced in little flickers of light on the grass. The park was quiet after the birds' dawn chorus had died down, even the zoo was unusually quiet. I left the den for my morning hunt. I chased a squirrel up a tree and was having a good bark at it, as it sat on a sunlit branch, high up, cheekily looking down at me. I saw Benni behind me, scavenging behind the kiosk. All of a sudden, a shadow fell over me. I turned around and looked up at a lady, with ginger hair and a boiler suit with words on[9]. She was holding a lump of cold sausage, my favourite, after warm sausage[10].

'Hello, little 'un,' she murmured soothingly, throwing me the sausage, 'have a piece of sausage.'

That's a no brainer I thought, gobbling it up. This beats barking at squirrels.

'Are you lost?'

I looked at her, she was holding another piece of sausage. I was a little bit suspicious because, although people having picnics would often give us food, I had never been offered any so early in the day. The lady threw the sausage near a yellow van. All inhibitions forgotten I chased it and ate it. Then I smelt another piece, yum, gobble, and another, yum, gobble, and another, yum, gobble. Suddenly there was a clang behind me. I turned around. Strange I thought, there's a mesh where I came in. No, I must have made a mistake. I turned around and around, trying to find my way out of this cage. There wasn't any. I was trapped. I barked and barked.

'Benni! Benni!'

'Benni, help, I'm trapped.'

---

[9] Of course dogs can't read otherwise Izzie would have known it said Ashby Dog Pound and, underneath, Warden.

[10] And after Dentastix, which is top of the list

'Mick,' the lady called out, 'I've caught the little, fluffy grey one.' She held out her hand with another piece of sausage. Her hand smelt doggy and then I realised what was happening. Yellow van. The dog wardens!

'Benni, run, it's the dog wardens, run!'

Just then Benni poked his head from behind the kiosk. Benni had been a survivor for months and could have run away but instead he came running at the dogcatcher, barking and jumping up at her. Benni wasn't a fierce dog but the dogcatcher looked alarmed and called out 'Down' in a really stern voice. Benni ignored her and continued barking and jumping, bouncing boisterously up at her.

Just then, Mick came running up with a cage and a noose for catching dogs. Benni was in danger too.

'Run, Benni, run. I'll be OK,' I called bravely and not being at all sure. 'Run!'

Benni ran, with Mick chasing him, but Benni was too fast and disappeared into the bushes.

Mick stopped, turned around and came back slowly, puffing.

'Come on, Isobel' called Mick, 'let's put this one in the van. We'll come back for the other one later.'

'So the tip from the lady having lunch in the park was right after all,' replied Isobel.

I realised then that the big woman having lunch on the bench was the reason I was caught. Grrrrr!

They lifted me and the cage into the back of the van. I growled.

'Come on, little 'un, we're off to Ashby Pound,' explained Isobel, 'you'll be given a good meal and a dry kennel and, hopefully, your owners will find you there.'

The van doors clanged shut. I felt trapped, alone and in trouble. I lay down, curled up and whimpered, and began to wonder what happened to dogs that went to the Pound. Benni had never seen a dog again after the Wardens had taken it away. I whimpered again. Would Josie and Joe find me?

Chapter 13 - The Pound

I was scared. The stressful drive to the Pound seemed to take a long time. The sun was on the right so we must have been driving north. Once I had finished whimpering I decided to bark, so I barked and barked. We stopped two or three times to pick up other dogs. At one stop Isobel gave me a dog biscuit, which I took and ate quickly in case she changed her mind. Anyway, I'm a dog and I'm always hungry. It was the least she could do after dog-napping me.

When we arrived at the Pound the van doors opened, and I couldn't believe my eyes, ears or nose. The place was full of dogs. Barking, yapping, sleeping, whining, each in a cage of its own. Carefully, Isobel reached in and put a choker lead around my neck and led me to a small cage between two other cages with dogs. On one side was a white Westie and the other a greyhound. I like Westies, they look like they are my cousins. As you know, I don't like greyhounds with their long, spindly legs and their 'mightier than thou' attitude. So I barked at it for a bit to show it who was boss, but I was pretty tired and stressed and soon lay down and had a chat with Westie.

'Where are we, Westie?' I woofed.

'A kennels, I think,' replied Westie, lifting his head off his paws. 'I've been here four days, it's like a hostel for dogs.'

'Oh.' I thought, I wonder what a hostel is? I was about to ask when my kennel door opened and two big hands reached in, put a collar on me, then a lead and pulled me out.

'Com' on, little 'un,' it was Isobel. 'The vet wants to see you.'

I don't like vets. Well, I mean I don't like going to the vets. As I write this I have learnt that vets are really nice people, they tickle my ears and chin and sometimes they even give me treats. However, I have learnt from experience that, normally, a visit to see the vet is bad news. The first time I saw a vet I was about six weeks old and living with Josie and Joe. He gave me an injection, which hurt a bit but wasn't too bad. The second time I saw a vet it was in the pound.

I was brought to a small room with a table at one side and cupboards on the wall. The vet had big bushy eyebrows, a bulbous nose and a big smile. He smelt of chemicals and dogs. He gave me a biscuit. Not a bad sort, I thought.

'Put her up on the table, please, Isobel.'

I hated being lifted up by strangers, so I growled and wriggled and wriggled and growled but it was no good, Isobel's grip was too firm. She put me down on the table, holding tight onto my collar so I couldn't wriggle. I looked over the edge, too far to jump.

'The poor little thing is trembling all over,' said Isobel, stroking my head and rubbing my ears. I liked that.

I have to say I was scared and trembling. I wasn't sure what was going to happen next. I wasn't even sure what a vet did, apart from stick needles into little dogs.

'Let's have a look at you, 'started the vet. 'Hmm, you have a sticky right eye that needs cleaning ....teeth...open!, that's it......fair condition, need a good clean, by the look of them you were born.....come on, open up...........born about February, so you're about five months old..........'. Isobel was taking notes, she

Page | 107

looked   up   and   winked   at   me.
'Paws......hmm..............OK...........fur and skin...............
nothing a good bath, groom and flea treatment won't
sort out.   Right, let's feel your body,' his big hands
wrapped around my waist and felt up my tummy, 'feels
fine there, bit skinny though, extra rations for you.'

He said this so cheerfully I thought it must be a
good thing.

'Right, let's take your temperature then weigh
you,' chuckled the vet.

'Hmmm,' he muttered a couple of minutes later
looking at a pointy stick thing, 'temperature's a little
bit high. Let's put you on the scales.'

He lifted me up and put me on another shiny metal
table. I tried to dive off, but he held on to me firmly
but gently.

'Six kilos, as I thought, a bit skinny. OK, Isobel,
kennel cough jab then back to the kennel with her.
Give her a bath, flea treatment, worm treatment, the
works. Try dry food and I'll see her in a couple of
days. Does she have a name yet?'

'No,' replied Isobel, 'when we found her she had
no collar on and she's not microchipped, I checked

before I came in. I thought we could call her Izzie after me, after all, she's the first dog I've ever caught!'

My ears pricked up to full alert. I couldn't believe she knew my name. I barked happily at her and wagged my tail. She stroked my head.

'Yes,' chuckled the vet, 'I think she likes that!'

I gave another happy bark. I began to think I would like it here.

'Look, she's wagging her tail like mad!'

And you know what? I was!

Chapter 14 - The Hearing Dog Scout

Life at the Pound was pretty good, once the first day was over. I didn't realise I needed so much attention to be a smart girl dog. After seeing the vet, I was given a bath. I had never had a bath before and I hated it, especially when they washed my face. I had always managed with a swim in the pond to keep me clean. Now I wriggled and yelped and squirmed and whined the whole time. A nice lady who smelt of lavender put me in a tub and squirted me all over with warm water, then started rubbing me all over with this foamy, lavender smelly stuff that made my eyes sting. Then, as if that wasn't bad enough, she squirted me with water all over again! I hate getting wet (except when chasing ducks in the pond) and I tried to shake the water off but she held me by the neck so I couldn't shake at all.

Then she toweled me down and I managed a big shake which sent water flying everywhere. She just laughed. Just when I thought it couldn't be any worse, she turned on a whirry thing that blew warm air at me. I hated the sound, just like a hoover, but it didn't seem too dangerous. Then she started cutting my hair short. I didn't mind this as I had a thick coat and it was quite warm. Once my hair was short, she picked up a spiky, toothy thing called a comb and started combing my hair, telling me she was removing all the unwelcome visitors she called little nippers. I had no idea what she meant but I did like the attention. All the time I was trying to dry myself by rubbing my face on the towel or her apron.

Well eventually she finished, to my relief. She took my photograph, just like Sinéad did except this time there was no gnome, and I was put back in my kennel. Westie came up and greeted me through the mesh.

'Phew. You smell awful, just like a lavender bush!'

He was right so I rolled over and over in my kennel to bring back some of that doggy smell.

The next day was warm and I started to settle in. Westie and I were allowed out together in a compound, so we played tag for a while. After that we were taken back to our kennels and given breakfast. Just before tea, after another run in the compound, I saw a grey Schnauzer being brought in on a lead. It looked like Benni.

'Benni!' I barked, 'it's me, Izzie.'

But it can't have been Benni as he ignored me.

At bedtime a warden I hadn't seen before came down the line of kennels, checking our water and giving us a bedtime time treat. She stopped at my kennel and threw me a bony treat, then looked at the name on my door.

'Ah, Izzie, I put your photo on the website this morning. Let's hope someone comes to claim you soon. Otherwise I might have to adopt you myself,' she winked.

I went to sleep thinking about what the warden had said. Would she really adopt me? She didn't even really know me.

On the third day, after midday snacks, a family came to look at the dogs. Walking down the passage was a woman with two small children, both girls. They followed a warden and were looking in the cages and calling 'Tricksie'.

Westie's ears pricked up, then she sat up.

'Tricksie,' called one of the girls.

Westie barked.

'Tricksie?'

Westie barked again and started scrabbling at the cage netting.

'There she is, mum!' called the taller of the two girls, running down to Westie's cage.

Westie was really excited, she was barking, jumping at the cage, wagging her tail and turning little circles in excitement.

'Yes, this is definitely Tricksie. See, she's missing the tip of her left ear, lost it in a fight.'

'Great!' exclaimed the warden, 'let's get him out. Have you got a collar, oh, you have, well done.'

He put the collar and a lead on Westie and turned to the woman as they walked back down the path.

'It's as well you came today. He was going to be moved on tomorrow. We only keep them for five days, you see. Now there'll be the fees to pay before you go. That'll be the Pound reclaim fee and four nights bed and board. For the fine we'll just call it the thirty euro for no collar and ID and ignore the others, as you have an up to date licence, don't you?'

'Bye, Westie,' I called

'Good luck, Izzie,' he called back.

Five days, I thought, five days! They'll only keep me for five days. Then what? I had been here three days and no sign of Josie and Joe. Benni's words came back to me, 'I've never seen a dog again after the Wardens have taken it away'. I started to tremble and I felt so lonely, I had no-one to talk to about it. The greyhound next door had kept its distance and we weren't on talking terms. I crawled into my den at the back of my cage and curled up on my bed, waiting.

On the fourth day, the greyhound went. No-one had come to collect her but a glum looking warden took her away. I think she sensed something was wrong as she tried to stay in the kennel. The other dogs were unusually quiet as she was dragged away. A poodle a few kennels down told us the greyhound had been a racing dog until she became too old and was left in a layby by her owner. I felt a bit sad I had barked at her on the first day and ignored her.

The day dragged on after that and I ate my dinner and bedtime treat without the usual excitement. What would happen if I wasn't claimed? As I thought about this I began to tremble again, and I whined myself to sleep.

The fifth day dawned, and I was sitting at my cage door, looking down the path to see if Josie and Joe were coming. A warden brought me my breakfast.

'You have a visitor today,' she told me, 'the Hearing Dog Scout no less. She'll be along this morning so look your best.'

A visitor, I thought, and a dog, not just any dog but a Hearing Dog called Scout? I didn't know what a Hearing Dog was, probably a rare breed but it sounded exciting, though I couldn't think why it would visit me! Anyway, I was still hoping Josie and Joe would find me. Patiently, I sat and waited.

Later that morning a warden and another lady came down the path. As they passed each cage the other dogs started barking a greeting, a sort of Mexican wave of barking as they walked towards my cage. They stopped.

'This is the other one we had in mind. She's been here five days so if no-one claims her today she'll need re-homing. We think she was born in February and has been a stray for a few weeks, so chances are her owners have given up looking for her. Her picture is on the website though.'

Given up, I thought! Could Josie and Joe give up looking for me? I suppose it was a long time since I had become lost, so maybe they had. Even so, I still had the rest of the day for them to find me.

'Izzie, this lady is the Hearing Dog Scout. She's going to look at you and decide if you'll make a good Hearing Dog.'

The Hearing Dog Scout, clearly not a dog after all, gave me an examination all over. She checked all the things that Izzy checked when she bought Lizzie. She was gentle yet firm. To be honest, I didn't mind the attention. She smelt of dogs so I thought she must be with them a lot.

'And you say she's coped well in the kennels the last few days? 'the Hearing Dog Scout asked, 'we need dogs who can adapt well to new situations and things.'

'Oh yes,' replied the warden, 'she settled in well and made friends with all the other dogs except, for some reason, the greyhound. And all the staff love her,' she added, smiling at me.

The Hearing Dog Scout looked me over again. I wagged my tail.

Finally, she turned to the warden.

'Sure, she'll be fine, she looks like she'll be a good candidate for a Hearing Dog. I'll be back tomorrow morning to sort out the paperwork.'

The warden locked my cage and I watched them go as they walked back down the passage. It wasn't too late for Josie or Joe to find me.

I waited patiently by the gate of my pen. The day dragged on and I carried on waiting until it was dark, the moon was high in the sky and the kennels quiet.

No-one came to claim me. I never saw my mum, Josie or Joe again.

Chapter 15 – My Trip to England

As promised, the Hearing Dog Scout returned after breakfast. I was given a new collar and led down to a small van and lifted into one of two cages inside.

'There you are, Izzie,' she said, 'have a drink while I go and fetch Daisie. She's going to be a Hearing Dog too.'

A few minutes later she came back with a golden spaniel.

'Hi, Daisie, I'm Izzie,' I introduced myself.

'Hi, Izzie, nice to meet you. This is an exciting adventure, isn't it? I love adventures. Don't you?' she beamed, as she sniffed around the cage and van.

'Right you two,' said the Scout, 'we're off to Rosslare to catch the ferry for England.' With that she shut the door.

'Daisie,' I piped up after a while, 'what is a Hearing Dog?'

'I heard they train clever dogs to alert deaf people to sounds, like the doorbell, alarm clock or fire alarm. The dogs help deaf people reconnect with life, they have even saved lives. The deaf people look after us and everything.'

'Oh, 'I murmured, 'sounds quite fun,' I added hesitantly, not quite sure.

'My cousin went deaf,' continued Daisie, 'she had trouble hearing commands, so her owner had to use sign language. Deafness can be a very isolating disability. The Hearing Dogs Charity has helped thousands of people already, they are really passionate about training us to do well. It'll be fun!'

The journey took all morning and my tummy was grumbling and telling me it must be snack time when we stopped. The van door opened and a strong smell of what I now know to be the sea came wafting in. Large white birds shrieked, swooped and flew around the sky. Daisie and I were put on the lead and allowed to jump down from the van and walk a short way. We were given a snack and a drink, and I looked around to see where we were. Lines of cars and other vehicles stretched away into the distance. People milling about, standing near their cars, chatting, waiting. A small girl pointed at me and Daisie.

'Look, daddy, 'oggy, two 'oggies,' she pointed.

Suddenly there was a loud HOOOT, which made me jump, and a voice could be heard all around us saying it was time to board the ferry. People started to climb back in their cars, and we were put back in our cages and driven on to the ferry, which turned out to be a very big boat. We stopped again and the van door opened. It was the Scout.

'You two have to stay here until the ferry docks in England. Here's some water for the trip. It isn't going to be rough so it shouldn't spill. It's not a long journey. I'll check on you later.'

And with that she dropped a treat in our cages, shut the door and disappeared. For a while there was a lot of noise, engines revving, shouts, clanks, bangs and chains rattling then, all of a sudden, it went quiet. A little later we felt a slight rocking motion which made me sleepy. I dozed off.

I was woken by the Scout opening the door and climbing into her seat.

'We're here. We'll be unloaded and in Fishguard in no time.'

Sure enough we drove off quite quickly and had only been driving a few minutes when we stopped again. The van door opened.

'This is where we part. Chloe from the Hearing Dogs will take you the rest of the way.'

Chloe was a bouncy young girl who gave us a big rub and tickle behind the ears. None of this sniff my hand business, just straight in. She had dark hair, grey eyes and a big smile.

'Nice to meet you two,' she chirped cheerfully, 'you're going to have such fun being Hearing Dogs. It's a real honour.'

This sounded good, I thought. I took an immediate liking to Chloe, I wondered if she was my new Top Dog.

We were allowed out, given some food and water and a little walk. I needed it. I didn't like being cooped up for so long. When we had finished, Chloe put us in a big van, separated inside into six transport pods.

Another long drive followed, longer than the one from Dublin to the ferry port. We pulled into a service area once for a break, a short walk and some food.

Eventually we reached our destination. The van stopped. We heard voices.

'Hi, Chloe, good trip?'

'No problems, they've been good as gold. Long day though.'

Telling me, I thought.

The van door opened. I could see the sun shining low in the sky, just over the horizon. The noise of a kennels filled the van, all sorts of dogs barking. They were telling each other that Chloe was back with more dogs. The noise and the smells were a little like the pound but somehow this kennels felt more vibrant, with a business-like, energetic air about it.

A shadow fell over me, I looked up to see another person standing next to Chloe.

'Which of you is Izzie and which is Daisie?' asked the new person.

'This is Izzie, Sarah,' explained Chloe, pointing at me. I woofed 'hi!', 'and this is Daisie.'

'Right, you two, welcome to the Hearing Dogs at Princes Risborough,' announced Sarah. We have some nice kennels for you in the Irish Block. Come on, it's late so we need to get you bedded down for the night.'

Daisie and I were led to a kennel block of four empty runs with cosy kennels and given one each, as well as a bowl of water and dinner.

'You'll be here for two weeks, just to check you're well and healthy before we give you to someone for socialisation,' explained Sarah.

I looked at Daisie. She looked at me.

'Sounds fun, it'll be a great adventure, I'm sure,' she beamed happily.

The next two weeks seemed to drag. There was only me and Daisie in the Irish Block so we became pretty good pals. We had a couple of visits to the vet, were taken for two walks a day, given an assessment of what commands we knew and were introduced gently into new situations, like the site restaurant where the smells made my mouth water. Even better, we were given some nice food and had a couple of toys to play with but otherwise it was pretty quiet. One bit of news did surprise me though.

We had been in the kennels for several days when Daisie came back from a walk with a volunteer.

'Hey, Izzie, I've just bumped into a spaniel in training and guess what?' she asked, carrying on before

I could say anything, 'he said it takes a year to be trained as a Hearing Dog!'

'A year!' I exclaimed, thinking back to the short sessions I used to have with Josie.

'Still,' I added, 'that's a lot of treats.'

'I know,' came the reply, 'he said we were like the Special Forces of the dog world.'

'Wow! What does that mean then?' I added.

'No idea, he wasn't sure either but that's what his trainer told him. Apparently we're the SDS – the special dog service.'

Towards the end of the two weeks we saw the vet again. Daisie left the next day. A couple of days later Sarah came to see me.

'Well, Izzie, the vet was pleased with you. Tomorrow you're going to your socialiser. What do you think about that, then, eh?' Sarah chuckled, tickling me behind the ears.

I woofed happily and wagged my tail.

'You're being transferred to the main kennel today. We have a new batch of strays coming from Ireland tomorrow.'

Chapter 16 – Ayla

The sun was streaming into my kennel early next morning, making funny shadows through the wire mesh of my new run. I was sitting ready and waiting to go to the socialiser. My toys were next to me. I was really excited. It would be nice to have a pack of my own again, although I would miss my friends at the kennels.

Sophie, my new neighbour in the kennel next door, came out of her den into her run, stretching her legs.

'Hello, Izzie, up already?' she yawned.

'I'm off to my socialiser today. Any minute I expect,' I replied.

'I know, you told me last night. It's very exciting.'

I heard the gate to the pound being opened and I moved to the mesh of my run so I could see who was coming. It was Sarah!

'It's Sarah, she must be coming to fetch me!'

Sarah's even footsteps came down the path and a few of the other dogs started jumping up and down and yapping. She stopped at my pen.

'Hello, Izzie, all packed and ready to go, then?' she asked, smiling her bright smile. 'You'll need your breakfast before you set off,' she added as she pushed a bowl under my door.

Never one to refuse food, I ate hungrily. Before you could say 'let's go' I had gobbled my food and slurped some water from my tin bowl. I sat up, wagging my tail and watching Sarah for the next command.

She opened the pen door, reached in and clipped a lead to my collar, picking up my toys as she did so.

'Come on, off we go,' she commanded.

I started to trot down the path after Sarah. The other dogs came out to see what was going on. Sophie pushed her nose up to her mesh.

'Bye, Izzie, we'll miss you. Have fun!'

'Bye, Sophie, have fun with your socialiser,' I stopped and rubbed noses, then turned to catch up with Sarah.

Her van was waiting on the other side of the gate, the rear door open. I jumped in and she shut the door. I shuffled over to the basket in the corner, hardly daring to believe I was going to a new pack. I hoped they would be friendly. It was so exciting.

The drive was quite long, and I dozed for a bit. After a while it started to feel bumpy, like we were driving down a road full of holes. The van stopped. I sat up and headed for the door, breathing in the new smells.

I heard Sarah climb out and she started to talk to a woman with a jolly voice.

'Hello, dear, have you brought Izzie?'

'Hi, Mrs Trotter, she's in the back, keen as mustard. Good as gold too,' she added, opening the door and letting the sunlight and smells stream in.

'Oh, do call me Penny, dear,' replied Mrs Trotter, putting her hand on Sarah's arm. 'And here she is,' she chuckled when she saw me sitting on the edge of the van.

'Woo-ooh,' I greeted her, wagging my tail back and forth across the van floor. Penny held out her hand for me to sniff. I dutifully did so – phew, strong perfume, I thought. She rubbed my ears and the back of my head. I knew we would get on well. I licked her hand then rolled on my back so she could rub my tummy.

'She's adorable!' exclaimed Penny dutifully, rubbing my tummy.

Just then a moving shape caught my eye. A cat! Skulking around the corner of a barn. I twisted and sat up, ears and tail up. The cat disappeared. I jumped out of the van to chase it, but Sarah was too quick, grabbing me by the collar as I landed on the ground.

'Oh no, you don't!' she exclaimed clipping the lead to my collar. I strained at the lead, whining and pulling. The cat was running away!

'I hope she isn't going to chase every cat she sees. We'll have to give her very strict training,' remarked Penny. 'Come into the house,' she added to Sarah, 'I'll put the kettle on.'

I took a last look at where the cat had been, then trotted after them. Maybe it would be great fun here, I thought, with cats to chase. I'll find and chase it later.

At first, I thought I was on a farm but soon realised it wasn't. It didn't smell of animals (except dogs and cats). Penny showed us the layout as we walked across the yard.

'This is the main house, dear,' she explained as we stood in front of an old, pretty, stone built, two story cottage, with blue painted bay windows and a solid oak front door with a huge brass knocker that looked like a paw. Pink and orange roses were growing under the windows. I sniffed one.

'I think she likes smelling the plants,' offered Sarah, nodding in my direction.

It's true I do. I like smelling lots of things.

'Over here, 'Penny continued, 'is the barn. This is where we make the cider from our apples.'

The door was open, and I could see lots of shiny tanks and things inside. It looked too much like a vet's surgery for my liking. I wondered what cider was. It certainly smelt nice, whatever it was. I could explore later.

'Over there,' Penny pointed at a long, cream coloured, single story building that made a third side to the yard, 'over there is the office, garage and stores and back here,' she continued as we went around the corner of the house, ' is the garden.'

In the garden was a golden-haired Labrador. I smelt her before I saw her. She bounded up to me and sniffed me. I skipped around behind her so I could sniff her in the way we dogs like to when first meeting a new dog.

'Let her off the leash, dear, the garden's fully enclosed, she can't escape.'

Sarah did as she was bid, and I scampered off with the Labrador in pursuit.

'What's your name?' asked the lab, 'mine's Ayla.'

'Izzie,' I answered back, making a sharp left turn then right to shake off Ayla, left again and then I was chasing her. We ran around for a while, Ayla in her lolloping way, as Penny and Sarah stood watching us, chatting and drinking their tea. Then Sarah turned to go. I went back to the gate to see her climb into her van.

'Ah-ooh, woof!' I howled. She turned and waved.

'Bye, Izzie, have fun, see you in two weeks I expect,' she called as she shut the van door. She drove off, bumping slowly down the lane and leaving a haze of dust behind her. Then she was gone.

I felt a wet nose on my flank. It was Ayla.

'You'll like it here,' she said, 'Penny's a good foster carer for pups being socialised. You're our fifth.'

Chapter 17 - More New Tricks

Well, I did like it there. I had a bed in the kitchen by the fire ('Don't lie too close or you'll singe your fur'), two nice meals a day ('My, you are a hungry one, always gobbling your food down'), snacks when Penny was cooking ('It's no good sitting there looking at me like that, any more scraps and you'll go pop') and cats to chase in the garden ('Haven't you got anything better to do than chase that poor cat?').

Penny told me I would have to learn to behave well in public places, so she took me on buses and trains, into shops and pubs and all sorts of places. We would walk along busy streets or busy roads. I noticed that Penny never dropped me in the deep end, so to speak, but always introduced me to new situations gradually. For example we started walking in a quiet street with a few cars, then a few days later a busier street, then later a very busy high street and once we walked along a four lane road that was so noisy I couldn't think straight and I was quite nervous, though I didn't like to show it as I'm a brave dog really. Penny was pleased with how well I coped with all the new experiences I met.

Every two weeks I was taken to puppy training classes at Princes Risborough Hearing Dogs centre where I had first arrived. These classes were fun because at the start of each session all the dogs were allowed to run around chasing each other, playing tag, rubbing noses and so on. There were only six of us, but it was very noisy! I had to be quite bossy with some of the other dogs, just so they knew it was me they were dealing with. After a while we would be called to order and given treats to calm us down before learning new commands and so on. Daisie was there too and Penny became friends with her socialiser, so we learnt things together. I re-learnt 'Sit!' – I still can't believe I earn treats just by sitting down – and learnt new commands like 'Heel', 'Lie down!', 'Come!', 'Walk on!', 'Leave!' and 'Leave, I said!'. In class I learnt that if I always paid attention to Penny's clicker and followed her instructions a small treat would follow. Many small treats make a tasty snack.

After class we would be taken into the restaurant on site where we all had to sit quietly while our owners chatted and had drinks and snacks. Usually we were given bits of toast or biscuit by some admirer.

After the fifth class there was a little ceremony where two dogs were given a one star certificate for their achievement. Penny told me that, if I did well at the next class, I would be awarded a one star certificate too. That would be real progress, she explained, and then I could go on to win the two star certificate that allowed me to wear the coveted Hearing Dogs red maroon jacket.

On the day of my sixth class I was very excited, as I hoped to win my certificate. However, when we arrived we were told that, instead of the normal class, we were going on a class outing into town. We all climbed into various cars and vans and set off for town. It was a fun day. We walked down the high street, lunged at a few pigeons, ran in the park, chased a few ducks, had a picnic, in fact it reminded me of the time I had spent with Benni in Dublin. I was still sad I would never see him again and hoped he was all right on his own. Perhaps he had found a new dog to be friends with. I hoped so.

The next week I won my one star certificate. I was so excited I ran around in little circles. Daisie gave me a well done lick and Penny gave me a big treat.

Being socialised by Penny, Ayla and Jim, Penny's partner, was fun. I was introduced to lots of new things and had lots of space to roam in the garden, though I wasn't allowed in the yard where I saw the cat the first day I arrived. We all settled into a new routine.

I remember my first Christmas[11], the Trotters had put up lots of lights and sparkly things all around the house and cheery songs played on the radio. They had some relatives to stay, two adults with two small children. They were all waiting for a very important person called Santa Claws (as we dogs call him) to visit on Christmas Eve. There was a big discussion about whether he could really fit down the chimney or should they leave the back door unlocked. It was decided to leave a mince pie and a glass of sherry on the kitchen table to entice him down the chimney into the kitchen. I waited up all night but nothing or no-one came, although the mince pie was tasty.

---

[11] A Dog is for Life not just for Christmas

In the morning the children were excited because the important person had arrived after all and left lots of presents around the Christmas tree. Penny and Jim were surprised that the mince pie had gone and looked at each other accusingly. I think Jim thought Penny had eaten it and vice versa, so I wasn't in trouble! Either way, they told the children that the important person must have eaten it but decided not to have the sherry as he was driving his sleigh. They explained the police were very strict on drinking and driving at Christmas, even for magical folk. The children weren't allowed to open their presents until after their breakfast, but I decided to investigate the presents under the tree.

Sniff, phew, strong perfume!

Sniff, sniff, chocolate, yum but I'm not allowed it as it can make me ill!

Sniff, ugh, pongy candle.

Sniff, sniff, sniff, aha! Smells like a doggy treat. I took the sparkly, gift wrapped package behind the sofa and clawed at it to open it up. A chew, I thought as much. I was just about to bite it when a shadow fell over me. I looked up, the chew held tightly between my paws. It was Penny looking over the top of the sofa.

'Izzie, what have you got there?'

I tried to hide the treat but too late. She reached down and took my treat.

'Hmm', she said, 'I suppose it has got your name on the gift tag so it is for you, but you were meant to wait until later so we could open the gifts together. You may as well have it now, but don't tell Jim!'

She gave me the treat, winked and disappeared. I ate my treat there and then before she changed her mind.

Later we opened the presents and I sat in the middle watching everyone open theirs in case there was another treat. In fact, Santa Claws had left me more presents – another chewy treat! Yum! And a squeaky toy. Ayla also had a couple of treats and a toy.

Later that day the Trotters were having a big dinner. I had smelt it cooking all morning and my mouth was watering from the smell. I sat in the kitchen hoping to have some. When they all sat down to eat, I sat by the table waiting for my bit of turkey and gravy. Ayla lay near the fire, warming herself. Suddenly the family started pulling noisy, loud, bangy things called crackers. Startled, I ran to hide behind the sofa. When

I looked out, I saw Jim pull out a little piece of paper, read it, look in my direction and say,

'Here's a good one,' he chuckled, 'how does your dog smell?'

'I don't know,' replied one of the little visiting persons.

'Through its nose, of course' added the other little visitor.

'No,' chuckled Jim, 'how does your dog smell? It smells awful, hah hah.' He roared with laughter.

Silly joke, even I know dogs smell with their nose.

'Here's another,' piped up a little visitor, 'can you guess what I am – here are a couple of clues. I have fore legs at the front and two hind legs at the back, making four legs all together.'

Everyone looked puzzled.

'Four plus two makes six, Jonny, not four,' explained Penny.

'Aha, I said fore – f-o-r-e – not four, and I bark.'

'You're a dog!' they all cried.

'Yup, just like Izzie and Ayla.'

After they had eaten, Ayla and I were given some of the dinner. It was delicious, meat, gravy, yum, sausage, bacon, yum, yum. I had lots. We were all so full we had to sit down and rest up in the lounge by the fire. Everyone was watching television except Jim who was reading a book.

'Uncle Jim, what's that book you're reading?' asked Jonny.

'Aunt Penny gave it to me. It's about people and it's called Men are from Mars, Women are from Venus.'

'If men are from Mars and women are from Venus, where are dogs from?'

'I'm not sure. Pluto, I expect,' came the reply.

'Oh, is that why Mickey Mouse's dog is called Pluto? Is he from Pluto?'

'I suppose so.'

'Then are Ayla and Izzie from Pluto too,' asked Jonny. Of course, I knew dogs were from the star Sirius, Benni had told me as much.

'They might be, no-one knows for sure, though Izzie was found as a stray in Dublin.'

'Is Dublin on Pluto?

'No, of course not, what do they teach you in school these days? It's in Ireland. Now, watch the programme.' Jim winked at me, reached into his pocket and threw me a treat.

Well, you get the idea, I loved living there and felt like I really belonged.

Little did I know how that was to change!

Chapter 18 - The Fire and My Assessment

Shortly after Christmas we had a disastrous event at the house, and I became the heroine of the family. Poor Ayla was at the vets after being hit by a speeding car on the road. She was going to be alright but had to stay in overnight as she had had a big operation on her leg. Anyway, it was late and I was alone in the kitchen after everyone else had gone to bed. I was a bit restless as I was missing Ayla. It was dark and the light from the full moon shone through the window, making slowly shifting, sharp-edged shadows on the kitchen floor. Every so often the shadows disappeared as a cloud drifted across the moon.

I must have dozed a little. I woke to a strange smell. I sniffed, then sniffed again to find out where the smell was coming from. I moved around the kitchen, still sniffing, the smell was strongest near the back door and it smelt stronger by the second.

I barked.

It became stronger. I barked again in alarm and went to the hall door, which was shut, and barked and scratched at the door. After a short while Jim opened the door and came in.

'What's all this racket about?' he growled, 'get to bed.'

I ran over to the back door, barking, and pawed it.

Jim frowned, 'what is it, Izzie?'

He came over to the back door, unlocked it and opened it. As he did so a bright orange light lit up his face.

'Oh no, the store's on fire! Penny!' he shouted, 'Penny, call the fire brigade.'

'What's the matter?' came the muffled reply from upstairs.

'The store's on fire, dial 999!'

Jim rushed out, grabbed a hose and started spraying the fire. I followed. The building was lit from the inside by the flickering orange light, streaming out of the windows and the cracks around the doors. Smoke was floating out of an open window and up the wall before following the line of the roof and blowing off into the darkness. The light and smoke from the fire were hiding the stars. The yard was filled with a crackling sound.

Penny came running past me from the kitchen. 'I've called them,' she shouted as she ran over to a tap on the yard wall and started filling a bucket.

'Here, I'll do that, you take the hose,' Jim ordered, handing Penny the hose and taking the bucket.

After a few minutes the hose and buckets seemed to be making a difference. Then the orange light was replaced by a blue light that became stronger. Two big, red vehicles roared into the yard and skidded to a stop. Alarmed, I ducked back into the kitchen doorway. Men in yellow clothes and hats jumped down and pulled out big hoses and sprayed the store. Before long the fire was out, and they started to clear up.

A tall fireman went up to Jim. 'Looks like we caught it before it spread to the other buildings. One crew will stay behind to do some checks. Any idea how it started?'

'No, luckily Izzie alerted us pretty quickly,' replied Jim, pointing in my direction.

The fireman looked at me, still sitting by the back door.

'Clever dog,' he grinned as he stooped down and patted me on the head with a big gloved hand. I wagged my tail.

'Treat?' I woofed hopefully.

'We'll leave this crew do their checks. Someone will come back in the morning to find out why it started,' explained the fireman. Then he left.

'Well done, Izzie!' exclaimed Jim, 'we'll find you a big treat in the morning.' Then he turned to Penny, 'It's a good job we sold most of the stock last week or it could have been a lot worse.'

'I know. The insurance should cover it. I'll call them in the morning. Meanwhile I'll see if these lads would like a cuppa. Come on Izzie, let's put the kettle on.'

We went inside.

The next day there were various people coming and going. Ayla came back in the afternoon with a big bandage on one of her hind legs. I told her all about the fire.

'Well done, Izzie,' she said approvingly, 'you are a clever dog. Shame I missed all the excitement.'

The following week I was due my first big assessment. When the time came Penny took me back to the Hearing Dogs centre at Princes Risborough as I had to stay at the kennels for two weeks to be assessed. Every day my assessor, Jim, would take me somewhere different, to town, on a bus, in the park, on a country walk or into buildings, like shops or pubs. He would check I would obey when he gave various commands. As the fortnight progressed, I thought I was doing well and expected the results any day. I was hoping to pass and then carry on to win my two star certificate.

The day of the results soon came round. Jim fetched me from my kennel and took me to the big training room (we dogs called it the drill hall) where we had our fortnightly training sessions. Penny, Jim and Ayla were waiting there for me. I greeted them enthusiastically. It was nice to see them again. They were pleased to see me too.

Jim sat down.

'Well, as you know this was Izzie's first assessment and I have taken her through all the usual checks. I must say she has come on a lot since she's been with you. I can see a real difference.'

Penny and Jim look pleased.

I wagged my tail. Ayla gave me a gentle nudge.

Jim continued, 'however, she has a number of traits that, I'm afraid, are still very strong, too strong for her to be a successful Hearing Dog.'

My tail wagging slowed.

'She's a brave and adventurous little dog but she has a very strong hunt and chase instinct, she can be over bossy and possessive. In my view we will always struggle with this so I'm afraid I have failed her.'

I saw Penny's face fall. My tail stopped wagging. Penny, Jim and Ayla all turned to look at me. Ayla put her paw on mine. My heart sank. I felt like I was falling down a deep hole.

'Oh dear, poor Izzie. I'm sure you did your best, Izzie,' exclaimed Penny soothingly, rubbing my back.

'What happens now?' asked Jim.

'We'll put her on the transfer list,' replied Jim, 'never mind, Izzie, even the best footballers go on the transfer list sometimes! We have people happy to adopt any dog that doesn't quite make it. We'll keep her here until she's re-homed. Here's a copy of her assessment card. She's a lovely dog, she'll make someone a great pet.'

Jim smiled at me and tickled me behind my ear.

'Don't worry, Izzie. We often have dogs that don't quite make the grade. We'll find a nice family to look after you.'

I tried to wag my tail, but it wouldn't wag.

Penny and Jim stood up to go. Penny stooped down and gave me a big hug.

'You'll be fine, Izzie, you are special,' she whispered in my ear. A little tear ran down her cheek and landed on my nose. I licked it off, it tasted salty, then I licked her cheek. She gave me a final rub behind the ears.

Jim patted me on the head, 'Be good, Izzie, I'm sure you'll be fine.'

Ayla nuzzled up, 'you'll be well looked after, it'll work out for the best.'

And with that Jim ushered them out of the door and they were gone.

I had never felt so alone.

Izzie's Assessment Report Card

	Dog: Izzie	Date: ███
Friendliness with people	Izzie is very friendly on and off site. People like her and she mixes well. She doesn't like being over fussed, though.	
Meeting other dogs	Izzie is good with most dogs but always barks at greyhounds and whippets for some reason. Can be bossy.	
Playing	She is not great at ball play and can be possessive with her toys. Her favourite game is chasing squirrels.	
Learning new experiences	Izzie is very good at dealing with new experiences. She fits in well anywhere and is a brave and adventurous dog.	
Responding to commands	Although she has her one star certificate she still has a very strong hunt and chase drive. She would lunge at pigeons in town and want to chase ducks and squirrels, even when called. Recall is patchy.	
Confidence	Izzie is a confident dog, if anything over confident.	
Public transport	She is generally good, if a little excitable at times.	

Around town	She can be a bit nervous around heavy or noisy traffic. Also, she is not very traffic aware and would happily chase a pigeon on the other side of the road if she could.
In public buildings	Izzie is generally good but can get fed up waiting and starts to whine. When eating out she will beg for food.
Overall assessment	Sadly, Izzie will not make the grade. She is very unlikely to gain her two star certificate and her hunt / chase instinct is too strong. She should be put on the 'transfer list'.
Assessor	Jim G.

Chapter 19 - My New Pack

I was sad when they told me I couldn't be a Hearing Dog. I quite liked the thought of helping people with hearing loss. I had good hearing and could tell the difference between a doorbell, telephone, alarm clock, cooker timer and lots of other beeps, dings, dongs, brrrrs and pings. But it wasn't to be. Jim had told me I was 'on the transfer list' and would soon be re-homed with someone who would look after me forever. I must admit, after some thought, that bit made me happy as my life up to that point had been very unsettled. It would be nice to stay with one pack forever, I thought.

Sarah took me back from the drill hall to my kennel. The other dogs started to bark so I barked back. Then I heard a bark I thought I recognised. I stopped to listen. Yes! It was, further up the line of kennels, I pulled Sarah along with all my strength to see. I pulled so hard the lead broke.

'Benni?' I shouted

There was a pause.

'Izzie? Is that you?' came the reply from further down the row.

'Benni! It is you!' I cried. I sprinted down the line of kennels, my broken lead trailing after me.

'Izzie, I thought I heard your bark. What are you doing here?' replied Benni, as we rubbed noses.

'I've failed my assessment so now I'm going to be adopted.'

Sarah came running up, panting.

'Do you two know each other?' she asked, 'I think you do, don't you. How's that, then? Izzie, you can go in this kennel next to Beamer.'

'Beamer?' I looked at Benni. Benni shrugged.

'I was a stray too, so they didn't know my name. That's why they call me Beamer,' he explained. 'Hang on, how do they know you're called Izzie?'

By this time, I was in the run next to Benni, so I explained everything that had happened to me since I last saw him in the park. 'Wow!' he kept saying and 'Really?'

When I had finished my story I asked him for his. This is his story.

'When you were taken away by the wardens, I went back to our den and hid for two days, only coming out in the dark for food and water. I did miss you, Izzie. After a couple of days, I decided to move den to a quieter part of the park, and I spent more time scavenging and less time begging bits of lunch off people. I only went up to those I thought I could really trust, like that nice family under the oak tree. They noticed you had gone, you know.

'During the next two to three weeks I noticed more stray dogs were disappearing so the wardens must have been busy. Then, one day, I met a dog running around the park with his owner. He told me that he had been a stray in Dundalk and had been caught and re-homed locally with a nice old lady, who treated him like royalty. It was then that I decided I had had enough of being a streetwise but lonely stray so do you know what I did, Izzie?'

'No, go on, Benni, tell me,' I demanded, hanging on his every word.

'I went to the park gates and sat there all day until the wardens came. They took me to a place called Aston Pound......'

'Me too,' I interrupted, 'that's where I was.'

'Well, they treated me nicely and looked after me for a few days, until a lady came and decided I would make a good Hearing Dog. Did you come over by ferry too?'

'I did. Oh, Benni, it's so good to see you again.'

We rubbed noses just like old times and chatted long into the night.

Two or three days later, as I was lying in my run, listening to the other dogs go about their training sessions and waiting for Benni to return, Sarah appeared at the mesh.

'Izzie, Chloe wants to take you down to Winchester to meet a lady who might adopt you. Come on!'

She opened the door and fastened the lead to my collar. Benni was still out training so I couldn't say goodbye. I followed Sarah past the other dogs. They were jumping up and down excitedly, asking all sorts of questions.

'Hey, Izzie, where are you going?'

'What's up, Izzie?'

'Will you be back later?'

We went through the gate. 'Here she is, Chloe,' called Sarah.

'Pop her in the back, please, Sarah. I'm taking Tinker to his new socialiser at the same time'

I jumped into the pod next to Tinker.

'Hi, Tinker.'

'Hi, Izzie, going to the socialiser too?'

'No, I've done that but failed the assessment so I'm going to be adopted.'

'Failed! I didn't know you could fail socialisation! How did you manage that?' questioned Tinker.

I told him. He laughed. That made me feel sad. Tinker could see my shoulders and ears sag.

'Sorry, Izzie, but never mind, I'm sure you tried your best and I bet being adopted is just as much fun,' he said.

The journey was uneventful except for Tinker muttering to himself every so often. 'Failed, I can't believe it. I'd better watch myself.'

Tinker was dropped off first. It reminded me of the day I was dropped off at Penny and Ayla's place.

Just as Tinker left I woofed 'Make sure you don't fail, Tinker!'

'Crumbs, I'd better not........I'll watch my step, thanks Izzie,' came the reply. 'Good luck!' and he was gone.

Chloe came back to the van. 'Next stop, Winchester,' she smiled, closing the door.

When the van pulled up at our destination I was sitting up, raring to go. The door opened and Chloe was standing there with the lead. I looked up and could see a three story town house.

'Come on, Izzie,' said Chloe as she rang the doorbell, 'let's say hello nicely to Sally.'

The door opened and there stood my potential new owner. She was smiling and looked friendly. I sniffed her feet. After introductions Chloe asked if I could pay a visit to the garden, as I had been in the van a long while. We went through the hall and utility room into a small fenced in garden with a little patio, some tubs and a few small plants and shrubs. I had a good look around for squirrels, rabbits, cats and other dogs – no sign at all – so I spent a penny and laid my scent to claim the territory.

Sally called me over.

I trotted up to her and lay on my back so she could rub my tummy. This is my way of saying let's be special friends. I also do it because I like my tummy being rubbed.

'She's lovely,' said Sally, 'though I hope she can manage all the stairs.'

That sounded like an invitation to explore so I dashed back into the house, through the hall and bounded up the stairs.

Sally and Chloe followed me into the house as I reached the top of the stairs.

'No problem with the stairs then,' I heard Chloe remark. I went into the kitchen – some nice smells there – through to a lounge-diner – good sized, full length window overlooking the front, I thought – back to the landing and up the next stairs. Bathroom, bedroom – pink, comfy looking bed, better not try it yet though – another bedroom – bigger bed – bathroom and a study. I ran back downstairs to the big window in the lounge. Great, I can sit here and watch the world go by and bark at any passing cats and dogs I see. Below me on the road was Chloe's van and across the car park area were more buildings, flats. People were walking through the car park, shoppers with bags, mothers with blue and pink buggies, school children in their green uniforms on their way home, jostling each other and laughing. Just then a dog and its owner came past, a Westie.

'Hi, Westie,' I woofed through the glass. Westie looked up and barked a greeting. I knew I was going to like it here.

'Oh, here she is,' beamed Sally poking her head around the kitchen door, 'she seems to like it here. Do you like it here, Izzie?' she asked.

Like it! I love it! I went up to her and wagged my tail. 'Ah-ooh.'

'Well,' agreed Chloe, 'that's settled.'

Chloe explained that Sally would need to come to the Hearing Dogs kennels at Princes Risborough to pick me up and sign the adoption papers. So, Chloe and I left but not before I had another tummy rub from Sally.

Over a week passed at the kennels with no news. I was wondering if I would ever be adopted. Benni told me not to worry, just be patient. Then, one Saturday morning Sarah came to my kennel.

'Izzie,' she called. I was in my den and poked my head out of my dog flap.

'Izzie, there's someone here to pick you up. You're going to be adopted.'

I bounded through the flap and up to the run door.

'This is it, Izzie!' cried Benni, 'goodbye and good luck, it was fun!'

My run door was open and Sarah was waiting with the lead. I stopped and turned to Benni. We rubbed noses.

'I'll never forget you, Benni. Thanks for everything, bye 'til next time.'

With that Sarah put me on the lead and I trotted down the line of kennels to the sound of a final 'wooo-ah-oo' from Benni.

I was taken to the drill hall. As I entered, I had a good sniff. Lots of dog smells and a new scent, Sally.

'Come on, Izzie, over here! It's no good sniffing around over there. '

Then I saw Sally and a new person sitting on chairs at the side. I trotted up to them, stood up and put my paw on Sally's knee, my new Top Dog.

'She's lovely,' exclaimed the new person, who I later discovered was Deputy Dog.

And that's how I came to be adopted by the Moss Pack.

Chapter 20 - Postscript

Now, as I write this book, I am part of the Moss pack. I'm not lost or a stray. I should say that I've never written a book before but luckily Deputy Dog helped me write this one. There are five of us in the Moss pack, me and four people, Top Dog (she's in charge), Deputy Dog (Top Dog's partner and best friend after me), their daughter, Dixie (Hot Dog) and her twin Dan (Mountain Dog). He's called that not because he looks like a St Bernard dog, which he doesn't, but because he loves mountaineering and rescuing people from crevasses. I'm the fifth member of the pack and, as you know, a girl, grey and furry, and a little terrier. Top Dog can't say terrier very well, she keep's calling me a little terror, but I don't mind.

We moved from Winchester and now live in a big den in Windsor, quite close to the Queen's castle. Although we often go for a walk near the Castle, I haven't seen the corgis yet. I expect they are very busy appearing at state visits and doing things like nipping the ankles of the Queen's guardsmen.

I have special places all around the house where I can rest or sleep or just hide away from all the hustle and bustle. Deputy Dog says we all need a quiet place like that – though I don't think he would fit into any of mine. I like to sit in the kitchen, next to the radiator, with a good view of the food preparation area so I can dart out and eat any food dropped (obviously I sniff it first to check that's it's not something yucky like lettuce – no self-respecting dog would eat lettuce!). Also, I love the smells in this room.

Outside is the garden. I'm allowed in the garden but only on a lead, because I kept escaping through the hedge at the back. One time I jumped over to the garden behind whilst chasing a cat. The grumpy lady who lived in the house behind our den wasn't very pleased to see me, in fact she was really cross. She threw a bucket of cold water over me and pushed me out through her gate into the street with a broom. I was quite frightened as I didn't know where I was. It reminded me of the time Mrs Goggins pushed me through Sinéad's gate and I thought I might be a stray again. I kept barking and eventually Deputy Dog came around the corner to rescue me. I was so relieved to see him.

Outside the garden is the Outer Territory. I often go for walks and hunts there with Top Dog or Deputy Dog. Territory is important to a dog. It marks out the area that we call our own and anything we find to eat is ours.

I love food. My three most favourite things are food. Here are my top ten favourite things, with my very most favourite at the top:

- Dentastix treats (other treats are available)
- Food that the rest of the pack eat, like chips, chicken, pizza or cheese
- Doggy food
- Sniffing things
- Chasing things
- My Pack
- Going for a hunt
- Having my tummy tickled
- Dozing
- Playing with my toys

There are a number of things I don't like. Here is my top ten.

- Fireworks and Thunder – these make me tremble and pant, I have to hide down Top Dog's bed until it's all over.
- Cats – they just deserve to be chased
- Hoovers and lawn mowers
- Heavy rain – this reminds me of the time I became lost
- Going to the vet – it's never good news, whatever Top Dog tries to tell me
- Big dogs with long legs, especially greyhounds (no surprise there!)
- Having my face washed and teeth cleaned
- Going to the groomer
- Being kissed too much or over fussed
- Other dogs sniffing my bottom

When I'm outside, hunting, I love chasing animals, especially furry ones, but feathery ones are good fun too. I am happy to chase big animals too, though I know now I'm not allowed to do this anymore. Once, when I was little and new to the Moss pack, I was out for a hunt with Top Dog and Deputy Dog in the countryside. They let me off the lead in a quiet field and I ran over a rise. There, in front of me, stood a deer. I'm not sure who was more surprised, me or the deer. I barked, it ran, I chased it. It bounded past a startled Top Dog and Deputy Dog, across the field and into a wood, closely followed by me, yapping away. I followed as fast as I could but when I came out of the wood, I could see the deer was getting away, so I stopped.

'Oh no,' I thought looking around, 'where are Top Dog and Deputy Dog?'

I listened. I could hear them shouting my name. Just then Deputy Dog came around the end of the wood, near the gate at the bottom of the field.

'Izzie!' he shouted angrily, 'Come here!'

Uh oh. I trotted over, sat down in front of Deputy Dog and received a good telling off. The pack are no fun sometimes, they should join in the chase!

Of course, it's more usual to find a cat or bird to chase. I find the odd hedgehog, but they don't want to play, they just curl up into a prickly ball.

When I'm out hunting, I play a game with Top Dog and Deputy Dog. We earn points for each animal we see. First one to spot it wins the points and the winner has the most points at the end. Points are awarded as follows:

20 points - each deer but, as you know, I'm not allowed to chase them. However, I do forget this sometimes. I am what Top Dog calls 'selectively obedient'.

15 points	- each hedgehog
10 points	- each rabbit or squirrel
5 points	- each cat
1 point	- large birds like ducks, fat pigeons etc. (small birds aren't worth chasing so don't count).

Farm animals like cows and sheep are not on the list as I'm not allowed to chase them. The best score near our territory is 22 (by Top Dog – four cats and two ducks) and the top score in the countryside is 50 (!!), also by Top Dog (one deer – un-chased, two squirrels, one rabbit). Top Dog really is an awesome hunter.

I have lived with my pack for some years now. My big adventures are over and life is pretty humdrum most days. We have our routines, I think my pack like their routines. I lie in front of the fire in winter, or sunbathe in the sun in summer. I go for hunts with my pack, I chase small furry animals and play tag with other dogs in the park. I'm given two square meals a day plus treats and nibbles, so I don't have to scavenge to survive anymore, although to be honest I've never lost that street habit. I am always on the sniff and look out for tasty morsels when out hunting. When Top Dog or Deputy Dog prepare food, I sit and watch them, and I'm often rewarded with a bit of meat or cheese thrown my way. Sometimes I'm given leftovers from their meals, my favourite is plum duck and venison steak. It took a while to train my pack to do this. It was only after numerous 'What? Biscuits? The others are having steak!' stares that they took the hint.

Top Dog looks after me nicely. She cleans my teeth and washes my face. She'll dry my paws when they're wet after hunting and give me a bath when I'm mucky.

I like to meet and greet Top Dog and Deputy Dog when they come back from work. They are both astronauts and work at the Space Academy. I come out from where I am and sit on the stairs and say 'wooooo-ahhhh,' then my tummy is tickled. I will come and welcome other visitors too, usually by sniffing their feet.

Last thing at night is another one of Deputy Dog's routines. It's my favourite one. He switches off the television and says, 'Come on, Izzie, time to spend a penny.' Off I go through the dog flap. Deputy dog opens the door and walks out (he's too big for the dog flap). He usually points out the moon, planets and stars for me, just like Benni did in the park.

One evening he said, 'see that tiny red dot to the left of Sirius, Izzie? That's Mars. Top Dog and I are going there soon to help set up the new base on the surface. It's where the new spaceships will be built for the mines.'

He said if I'm good and clever I could be a highly trained, specialized space dog working on one of the space barges going to the asteroid mines. Benni would like that.

When we come back in Deputy Dog gives me a Dentastix. I jump into bed and eat it, my favourite! That's a dog's life!

At least I thought it was, but then I became an astrodog and my space adventures started........

If you liked this book, watch out for Izzie's next adventure …..

Izzie and the Martian Adventure

Having travelled from Dublin to be a Hearing Dog but failing to make the grade, Izzie takes on new adventures with the Moss Pack. Her pack are astronauts and she wins the chance to be a highly trained, specialised space dog. At the Space Academy, she helps solve the theft of the secret ion drive design, but tough training and more assessments lie ahead. A tragic event leads to a flight to Mars with Dixie, her handler, where a bigger, more sinister mystery awaits. But are her skills up for the job? Can she help find the criminal mastermind before it is too late? And does she really have a doggy spacesuit? Find out by reading *Izzie and the Martian Adventure.*

Due out at the end of 2019…………………

Thanks

Thanks to my wife Sally who encouraged and supported me when writing this book and made many suggestions, and to my daughter, Sarah, who read it to her Year 2 class and then invited Izzie and Deputy Dog into school for a 'Meet the Author' afternoon, which involved lots of treats (at least for Izzie).

The lovely little sketches of Izzie were done by Grandma Shirley, who loved animals.

I wish to acknowledge the help from David Robson and Tom Green of the Hearing Dogs for Deaf People Charity. David reviewed the text and Tom gave me advice about the selection and training processes for hearing dogs. The Charity's processes have moved on a lot since Izzie was at Princes Risborough. Due to improved selection and breeding processes, dogs are no longer brought over from Ireland. Socialisation and assessment processes have also been developed and improved.

Thanks also to my PA, Denise Read, who proof read the final draft and Gautier Jacob, a colleague at work, who said, 'of course I would like to read it' and did so and encouraged me to publish.